Misunderstood

NOTHING TO JOKE ABOUT

Misunderstood

⚡ NOTHING TO JOKE ABOUT ⚡

JAY SHERFEY

iUniverse LLC
Bloomington

MISUNDERSTOOD: NOTHING TO JOKE ABOUT

iUniverse books may be ordered through booksellers or by contacting:

iUniverse
1663 Liberty Drive
Bloomington, IN 47403
www.iuniverse.com
1-800-Authors (1-800-288-4677)

ISBN: 978-1-4917-0110-2 (sc)
ISBN: 978-1-4917-0111-9 (e)

Library of Congress Control Number: 2013913630

Printed in the United States of America.

iUniverse rev. date: 08/19/2013

Again with heartfelt gratitude, I want to thank,

- My wife, Claudia, my daughter, Kirstin, and my son, John for the alone-time I needed to finish this work.

- My sister, Sara, who offered valuable feedback.

- My friends at restaurants where most of the writing was done who read and offered advice.

- The good people at iUniverse who pleasantly drove me to make the final revisions. The book is better.

- My writing mentor, Fran Bellerive, who has been nudging, cajoling, guiding and editing this story from the beginning. I could not have made it without her.

Prologue

May 1964

Doctor Hiram Lipton slept poorly. Abandoning the bed at daybreak, he splashed cold water in his face and through his short, white hair. In the bathroom mirror, unmistakable signs of stress showed in dark patches under his eyes. The reality of his offer to get Jason Sutter to New York shook him.

Lipton, a psychiatrist, worked with patients in the small towns and hamlets south of Philadelphia. The doctor met the psychotic, thirteen-year-old Jason Sutter last year in the late winter. He concurred with the diagnosis. By the beginning of the public school's summer vacation, however, he did not know what to think. The boy seemed to have healed himself.

Lipton leaned on the sink and shook his head with the memory. The cure bewildered him. Never had such a thing happened with this diagnosis. He checked his watch. In five hours he, a reluctant driver at best, would be at the Dubois house to take Jason to his mother.

Jason lived in a specialized foster home for only the worst cases. Lipton used his professional connections to make inquiries about Jason's family. To his astonishment, Jason's mother, Elizabeth Sutter, was discovered in the care of a New York State mental hospital.

"A promise made is a promise kept," the doctor reminded his reflection in the mirror. He dressed, packed, and went to the kitchen.

Anxious to stop thinking and get going, Lipton walked out to the garage. A beige blanket covered his car like a fitted sheet. He pulled a corner of the cover and lifted it off his shining black Mercedes sedan. Then he folded the blanket and put it on a shelf behind him and got behind the wheel. The engine started and ran with a steady rumble.

"Maybe I'll just practice driving for a while . . ." This sort of nervous, one-sided conversation was reserved for activities Lipton tended to avoid. He got out and lifted the garage door.

"Oh, don't worry. I'll drive you," he said, mimicking his promise to Jason. The boy's grateful reaction had kept his thinking brain from engaging. "No problem, just hundreds of terror-stricken highway miles." The Mercedes rolled smoothly onto the driveway. The doctor went back into the house, mumbling, "Just shoot me now."

Lipton double-checked the locks, the lights, and anything that should not be left on and then grabbed his bag. Once it was in the trunk and the garage door clattered closed, he took the driver's seat and a few deep, shaky breaths. The sedan rolled in reverse into the street, abandoning the safety of the driveway. In minutes, its driver guided it into morning traffic. Sweat beaded on Lipton's forehead as he shared the road with those other certifiably insane drivers.

By late morning, with the sun bright in a cloudless sky, Jason Sutter rode in the passenger seat with the window down. He loved the fresh air as it rushed by his face. His hand ran over the leather seats: so much room. *Now, this is luxury*, he thought as he stretched his legs. His new sneakers, Converse high-tops, and his New York University sweatshirt—gifts from Frank, his foster father—made him feel special. His eyes danced over the switches and dials and then settled on his guardian for this trip to New York.

"You all right, doctor?" he asked, concerned with Lipton's condition.

"Fine, Mr. Sutter." The older man's hands, white knuckled, clenched the wheel.

"You don't look so good, sir." Jason had not seen his former therapist since the silencing of the voices echoing in his head.

The doctor's hunched posture looked painful. His eye's sought for any sign of imminent disaster, never resting. This behavior was so unlike the relaxed man behind the desk with a smoldering pipe in hand.

"Well," Lipton said. He pushed his face closer to the windshield. "I'm not used to highway driving. I don't get much practice, you see." The doctor drove north five miles below the speed limit. Cars backed up behind him. The long line of cars was like a long line of grocery shoppers with only one register working, Jason thought. When other registers open, the queue of impatient and angry customers dissolve as customers dash to cash out and go. Horns and voices raged as the delayed motorists passed Lipton.

Jason looked away from his friend's discomfort. A mix of industrial and natural landscapes flew by the open window. Not psychotic, but a gifted telepath, Jason had learned through tough experience how to control the thoughts broadcasted from people nearby. His good friend and doctor, cringing at the wheel of the car heading north, had created the opportunity to reconnect with his mother. Lipton could not begin to understand the depth of his gratitude.

"I think . . ." Jason said after a time, "that you should call me Jason." He turned away from the window and added, "I'll call you, Doc. Okay?"

"Yes, yes. That would be fine." Lipton's right eye twitched and blinked. It needed a scratch, but he knew something bad would happen if he did. He would trade almost anything for a seat not moving at fifty miles per hour, a full pipe, and good conversation.

"So, Doc, thanks for giving me this lift."

"Well, Jason," Lipton said. He grinned for the first time since the car had pulled away from the curb. "It isn't every day that you get to accompany a certified fourteen-year-old genius." Momentarily distracted, his shoulders relaxed and his right hand relinquished the wheel. He quickly wiped his irritated eye. "Considering where we started, this outcome was not expected, eh?" Lipton recalled his work with Jason when he entered the Dubois foster home. It was a time when Jason pounded walls. "You never did tell me how any of this came to be." He stole a quick glance at his passenger.

Jason sensed an easing in the doctor's fearful condition.

"It's a long story, Doc." Jason had expected this question, and he planned to work the angles. How much could he tell this good man and not put him in danger? Their destination was the center of the enemy's fortress. From New York City had come the psychic attack that almost killed his best friend's sister. An errant thought could bring the wrath of the gods down on them both.

"Time, my boy, is exactly what we have right now." The doctor's shoulders relaxed further with the expectation of a good telling. "Humor an old man."

Jason sighed. "You ever hear the name Newton when you worked with patients in Kearny, or maybe you follow local school sports in Franklin Chase?"

"No to both, my boy," said Lipton. "Chess is more my sport."

"You have to understand Newton and football, or the story will make no sense." Jason stared out of the window, remembering what he had learned since last September at the start of the school year. The day of the school football team tryouts seemed like a good place to begin and help the good doctor catch up: the tryouts and the mysterious visitor.

"You were saying, my boy," Lipton said, pulling Jason back from his thoughts. The doctor settled back in his seat. "Please explain."

"It all started in September on the field . . ."

Chapter 1

September 1963

O f all the possible foods in the world, Jason never thought fertilized dirt and grass would be on the menu. He lay spread-eagle facedown on the thirty-yard line of the McKinley Middle School football field, his helmet's face guard buried in the turf. The wind had been knocked out of him, so he remained still, trying to breathe. Everything hurt. The team tryout session had started an hour before. It felt longer.

A few weeks earlier, fearing attack from powerful psychics, Jason had modified memories of people living in a twenty-mile radius of Franklin Chase. He was desperate to be known only as a regular kid and to have a normal life. The long-distance assault never came, but he prepared for a scout showing up in Franklin Chase who must find nothing in anyone's mind revealing his secret. His foster father, unaware of Jason's mental talents and concerned about the boy's sudden worried and serious demeanor, suggested football to help his further recovery; they started training together. Since the start of the school year, Jason had not used his telepathy in any way.

"Good hit!" someone standing close by said with a laugh. Jason could see black cleats. His eyes rolled left and right. Others gloated over his prostrate body. "Another seventh-grader bites the dust." They laughed and walked back to the defensive huddle called by Logan, the middle linebacker who had knocked Jason flat.

"Hey!" Jason panted. He lifted himself onto his hands and knees and pulled a grass-encrusted dirt clod from the helmet's grill. He spit and stood on shaky legs like a newborn foal. His white jersey and gold pants showed grass stains that looked more like green tire tracks. The defense team turned around.

"In case you didn't notice," Jason said as he tossed the ball to the assistant coach, the referee for the tryouts, "I caught and held onto the ball." Jason spit again, trying to get the dirt out of his mouth.

"Son of a . . ." Logan shook his head in disbelief. "I nailed that little punk." He looked to the sideline, where the head coach, Mr. Gunther, tilted his head in a "What happened?" way. It was the older boys' assignment to discourage the young kids, the seventh-graders. Logan shrugged and turned back to his players.

Jason smiled and saluted Logan and then hobbled back to the offense huddle for the next play. The other twelve- and thirteen-year-old boys who had not been rolled over and tossed aside joined the huddle exhausted, hardly able to breathe. There were five left. They looked around afraid. Only Jason and another seventh-grade boy named Arthur Robinson seemed anxious to get their hands on the ball. Arthur knelt on the sidelines, waiting his turn.

Rodger Bachman, the quarterback, looked to the sideline for the next play. He grinned and nodded at Mr. Gunther. "Same play," Bachman said. "You ready, Sutter?"

Heck, no, Jason thought. This was not the best time to be a normal kid. A telepath, he struggled every day to set aside his gifts. Not long ago, he had discovered that there were others like him—but dangerous. He had to hide. Using his power would be like sending up flares signaling his location. It would be so easy to change the play with a thought. Jason shook his head, determined to hold his normal ground.

Bachman snickered. "You better be ready." He thought Jason was scared, ready to quit.

Jason planned his own variation on the play. After working with his foster father on moves and strength training for the last four weeks and now being quick and strong, he knew that the next hit would be worse than the last. With the ball secure in his grasp on the last play, a gauntlet had been thrown down. It taunted Logan. The middle linebacker would pick it up and slam him with it. Jason watched him moving behind the defensive line, calling out assignments, and he smiled.

"Thirty-nine wide on three," said Bachman.

"Break" called the huddle. Hands slapped. Jason broke from the circle, determined not to go down without a fight. He stood ready a few yards to the right of the tight end. The call required him to fake right and then slant across the middle. A good fake maneuver would confuse the defense unless, as in this case, they knew what was coming.

"Forty-two, forty-nine," called Bachman. "Thirty-nine wide. Hut, hut . . ." The ball slapped into his hands. He stepped back into the pocket behind his linemen. He cocked the ball, faked right, and then drilled the ball to Jason, who was crossing midfield at full speed.

The ball bounced off Jason's left shoulder pad as he lowered his head and like a bulldozer slammed into Logan's breadbasket. Logan's greater weight pushed Jason back, but he planted his cleats hard into the turf. Jason crouched, changing his center of gravity enough for Logan's weight to be sent up and over. The linebacker flipped, sailed about ten feet, and landed on his back.

"I'm inexperienced, not stupid." Jason knelt by Logan as the whistle sounded. He undid his strap and removed his helmet. "Remember that." He stood and stormed to the sideline, where he stopped in front of Coach Gunther and said angrily, "If you don't want us, just save us all a lot of trouble and say so!" Disgusted, he threw his helmet on the ground at Gunther's feet.

The old man ignored him. He focused on the field and signaled another play. With no reaction from the coach, Jason moved off and planted himself on the bench, furious.

"Time," called the ref, who then trotted over to the sideline. "Logan's passed out. You wanna keep going?" Gunther nodded. The defensive players hauled Logan from the field.

"Robinson!" The coach pointed to the only dark-skinned boy trying out. "You're in for Sutter. Collier! Cover for Logan." Collier headed onto the field, pulling on his helmet.

Arthur "Artie" Robinson jumped up smiling, put on his helmet, and ran out to the huddle. He and Jason were the same age. Artie had missed a year or two of school due to physical ailments, as opposed to the mental illness, misdiagnosed, that slowed Jason's academic progress.

In the first days of school, they became allies against their teacher, Mrs. Hatcher. On the first day she made it clear that she thought Jason and Artie should be with the slow students, since they were so much older than the other children. Artie racked up one more negative. "A Negro in my classroom cannot possibly succeed." Mrs. Hatcher, her dark hair done up in a tight bun, stood over him, tapping a ruler lightly against her palm. "I am not one of those who make it easier on those who have had it so bad. We've all had it bad, one way or another."

"Yes, ma'am." Artie nodded, a serious expression on his pleasant face.

"The same for you, Mr. Sutter." She tapped her foot in time with the ruler.

Jason wondered if she knew his foster mother, who had a habit of tapping her foot when annoyed. He spent most of his time at his foster home defending himself from his foster mom, Lydia Dubois, who took pleasure in others' pain. She had almost discovered Jason's abilities, which would have been a disaster. Lydia enjoyed using people, especially the emotionally wounded, to build her financial fortress. Frank, his foster father, started out as one of Lydia's dependable tools, but then Jason showed up. Frank changed. It was not clear what would happen next in Frank and Lydia's relationship.

"You shouldn't be here either, Jason," insisted Mrs. Hatcher. "I'll be keeping my eye on the two of you. If you show any signs of falling behind, you will be changing classrooms."

"Yes, ma'am," said Jason, following Artie's lead.

Mrs. Hatcher's complaints stopped after two weeks when neither boy had any problem with the material she taught. When they wound up on the list to compete for a position on the football team, Mrs. H found another reason to complain. "Experience has taught me that you can't be banging your heads up and down a football field and be good students." Her foot tapped the floor. "I will not make allowances."

"Yes, ma'am," the boys said together.

On the football field during tryouts, Artie took his stance. The quarterback called the same play. Jason threw up his hands in frustration. Where the ball had hit Jason in the shoulder pads, it zoomed over an empty field until a hand reached up and pulled it down. The defenders crashed into each other over Artie. He shot out from under them and tore down the field to score a touchdown.

"Well, all right!" shouted Jason, jumping to his feet, clapping hard. "Way to go, Artie!"

"How the hell . . ." Collier pulled himself off the ground after colliding with the safety going after Robinson.

Coach Gunther waved over Bachman. He whispered in his ear and then slapped his shoulder pad as his quarterback went back to the huddle. Jason wondered what was going on.

For the next play, Artie lined up as a wide receiver instead of in the slot as Jason did. When Bachman took the ball from the center, Artie shot down the sideline, stopped, turned around, but did a three-sixty spin. Surprised, the cornerback stopped; he looked for the pass. Artie flew passed him. Bachman threw the ball with all his might. It sailed, and hung in the air. As Artie stole a five-yard lead on the closest defender, he slowed to get under the ball and caught it easily. He crossed the goal line, trotted calmly back to the huddle, and then tossed the ball, as Jason had, to the assistant coach.

After running a few more patterns, with Artie catching every ball thrown his way, Coach Gunther called the tryouts finished. For those who stayed on the field the entire time, Gunther said, "We'll let you know in a week or so. If it doesn't work out this time, you might make the team next year. Don't give up."

The older boys jogged into the locker room, laughing. The younger boys followed, moving slowly with hang-dog expressions. They knew they would not make the team.

Jason walked with Artie. "What do you think?"

"Don't rightly know, man," said Artie. "The coach is a hard man to read. Doesn't give anything away." He looked back over his shoulder, seeing Gunther talking to his assistant. "I think we got a shot."

After changing, they walked together to the front of the school, where Jason's foster father waited in his blue Valiant.

"You want a lift home?" asked Jason.

"I don't think your dad is all that thrilled about driving me around." Artie looked at the man waving to Jason to hurry.

"Yeah, I know." Jason stopped and turned to Artie. "Let's see if we can get you close. Okay?"

"I won't turn down a lift, if I can get it." Artie clapped Jason on the back. "Thanks, man."

Artie watched as Jason approached the car and then leaned in the passenger-side window. Jason's right hand pointed at him. When Jason threw down his book bag, Artie thought the negotiation was not going well. Artie wanted to tell him to let it go; it wasn't that far to walk. Artie was used to a lack of consideration from white folks.

Finally, Jason pulled back from the window, opened the back door, and waved Artie over. He grabbed his bag and threw it in as his friend jumped in the back. Jason took the front seat.

"I'll drop you at the train station," stated Frank curtly. He kept looking around to see if anyone saw him giving the boy a lift. He checked the mirror repeatedly.

"Sure, Mr. Dubois, that would be fine." Artie smiled. "Thank you, sir."

"How'd it go today?" Frank started the car. He glanced at the mirror and then asked Jason, "You think you made the team?"

"We sure didn't make any friends today." Jason winked at Artie. "Artie here caught a long ball and scored even though the backs knew what was coming."

Frank nodded and smiled. "Well, that is something." He appreciated speed and had worked hard with Jason to instill the notion that in football the victory goes to the quick more than to the large. "It's hard to stop what you can't catch."

"Yes, sir." Artie smiled. "My dad and me work on that all the time."

"What kind of practicing techniques do you use?" Frank looked at Artie in the rearview mirror.

"Sometimes," Artie said, "he has me wear a backpack full of stuff to slow me down. We throw and run the ball in a field near our house, and I have to be as fast I can."

"Jason and I do something similar," Frank said. "What about . . ."

Frank's sudden wealth of words surprised Jason. His foster father had made it clear that he did not want to be the local transportation for anyone else, especially a colored kid from that other part of town. Now, however, he and Artie were on the same plane, talking football.

Neither noticed Jason as he sat up rigid, shocked. He stared ahead. A black Cadillac was approaching in the oncoming lane. Jason felt the mental pressure build: a probing that pushed on his consciousness. He concentrated on football and what Artie said to Frank. The Cadillac passed them without slowing. Jason turned and watched the car disappear in the distance. The dangerous others had arrived in Franklin Chase.

"Yeah, Mr. Dubois," said Artie, agreeing about the hard work needed to overcome differences in size. "Uh . . . Mr. Dubois?" He watched the train station go by. "You were going to drop me off back there?"

"Oh hell!" Frank slowed the car. "Well, why don't you just point me to where I can drop you."

"You're coming up on my house, so anywhere along the way here is fine."

Frank pulled the car to a stop at the side of the road. Artie jumped out and thanked him for the ride. "See you tomorrow, Jason." Artie smiled and headed to the nearest house.

"I like the way that kid thinks." Frank watched him walk to the small, single-story, white clapboard house. "I first thought you and him were competing, but what a combination you would make. I hope Gunther is not blind to the possibilities." When Artie disappeared through the front door, Frank put the car in gear and turned it around. Jason remained silent; he needed a plan. The driver of the black Cadillac scared him.

"Jason?" Frank turned to look at him. His foster son looked over at him. "You okay?"

"Oh, yeah." Jason decided to focus on the tryouts. "Don't get your hopes up. I yelled at the coach. I wasn't happy with what was happening."

"What was that?" Frank slowed as he approached a red light.

"They kept running the same play. The defense was killing guys 'cause they knew what was comin'. Kids were getting hurt." Frank chuckled, and Jason stared at his foster father, fuming.

"You're in, my boy." Frank slapped the steering wheel. "You made the team. Gunther wants players with spunk and talent. Just you wait and see."

✧   ✧   ✧

The black Cadillac sat parked in the shadow of a large oak tree, its driver apparently sleeping inside. The neighborhood kids passed it on the way to play ball after school. When it was there on their way home, they wondered if the guy behind the wheel was dead. A quick debate behind the nearest tall hedge settled the matter. The boys would sneak up from behind.

Bill Sorenson, very much alive, ignored the youthful scrutiny. His attention was on the house ten blocks away. When he wanted, he saw the world in a spectrum of psychic energy. His wife, Reena, glowed a bright, golden yellow unless she did not want to be found. She was the top authority and only member of the Community that could hide from his ability. Her orders were simple: find any telepaths outside of Community control and verify that the kill order had been carried out. She waited patiently in Bismarck, North Dakota, for her husband's report.

Bill relaxed and released his special vision. Ungifted humans, animals, and inanimate objects registered in shades of brown. Anything touched with psychic energy radiated for a time, depending on the strength of the absorbed energy. Bill was adept at reading the signs and knowing the difference.

The house capturing his interest glowed bright green. Bill looked down on it as though he hovered above. Their neighbors' homes to the right and left were brown. This was the place Rodney Davenport, the Northeast Community leader had reached out from his fortress in New York City and focused his power; it should have snuffed out the significant psychic power found outside of the Community's control. Reena Sorenson had sensed the independent power when scanning the mid-Atlantic states from her

Midwest home and had ordered the strike. It was standard procedure. After months, the house still radiated. Rodney's attack had been very strong.

When Bill arrived in Philadelphia from North Dakota in August, he feared the energy had dissipated, leaving no readable signature. Reluctantly, Rodney, a thorn in Reena's side and a constant complainer, provided a target area when Bill contacted him from the airport.

"It wasn't Philly. Somewhere south. Maybe twenty or thirty miles. A small town—" Rodney sneezed. He took his time wiping his nose and then said, "That's all I got." He hung up.

Bill had trawled for the location of the attack, rolling down the streets in the towns south of Philadelphia. Halfway through September he drove into Franklin Chase, where his instincts immediately registered some activity, and his search began in earnest.

As he watched, focusing from above, people walked out of the green, glowing house into the backyard. One of them, the larger, was a dull red clearly generating a low-grade psychic energy. The smaller was as dark as the surrounding houses. What bothered Bill was the edge of yellow trim surrounding the smaller of the two objects. He knew it was the youngest child. Days earlier, he had visited the house in the guise of a salesman, looking for families with small children to whom he might sell swings and slides.

"Oh," said the woman who answered the door. "There is only our daughter Patti, under the age of ten."

"Well, thank you anyway, Mrs. . . . ?" Bill raised an eyebrow and extended his hand.

"Wyatt. Mrs. Wyatt." Peg smiled, hesitated, but shook his hand out of courtesy. Something struck her as wrong. When Bill said his last thank-you, the door slammed and the dead bolt shot home.

Bill stared at the door a moment and then picked up his bag and turned away. He headed to his car, surprised to find a psychic in this backwater town. Her capabilities were minimal but recognizable. More important, the little girl lived. Rodney had failed to eliminate the threat. This failure bothered Bill. Was Rodney simply sloppy, or had he been duped by a more powerful psychic? So far Bill found no evidence of another power in the area. *The girl might be a normal*, he thought. *Rodney has connived against Reena long enough; he needs to be replaced.*

"Maybe we have cause at last, my dear," he whispered to himself, imagining Reena's smiling face. Getting rid of Rodney had moved to the top of Reena's list in the past few months.

Bill watched the figures play in the backyard. Three other dull, red objects came out of the house. The fourth and last to exit had a dull-orange glow brighter than Mrs. Wyatt's. Bill sat up in the seat, ending his search and observation session. *It may be nothing*, he thought.

"But it may be everything," he muttered aloud. He needed Reena's inputs before he took further steps. His hand grasped the key in the ignition. The engine roared to life. The boys squatting behind the vehicle trying to decide how to approach the unconscious or dead driver jumped up and ran for the nearest cover.

"Sorry. Boys." Bill laughed and watched them scurry. *What fools these mortals be*, he thought as he launched the Cadillac from the curb.

✴   ✴   ✴

After dinner, Suzy met Jason in the toolshed in the Dubois backyard. Six months earlier, when he had escaped the haze of the heavy medication for his misdiagnosed psychosis, Suzy, another foster child in the Dubois house, had befriended him and helped him relearn how to read, because his memory had been wiped clean. When Jason did the same thing to Russ's sister, Patti, to hide her after the psychic attempt on her life, he figured that his mom had done the same to hide him from very dangerous people. The problem, of course, was that Patti Wyatt had her brother, Russ, and Jason to keep an eye on her. Jason stood alone.

The toolshed, where he had lived until he gained better control of his wall pounding, was now their official meeting place. He felt comfortable within those weathered pine walls. Suzy and his best friend, Russ Wyatt, a freckled-face, red-haired idea dynamo were sitting at the bench, ready to help Jason work a plan for what he could do and how he might protect himself. Russ set his friend on the highest, superhero pedestal after he saved Patti. And the three of them had become a unit; like the Three Musketeers, they helped one another any way they could. Russ offered his zany—but in the end, good—ideas, and Suzy provided thoughtful, practical suggestions.

When Jason had gained control of his abilities, he found Suzy's thoughts blocked to his incursions, unlike most other people's. This was important, but he had no way to discover why. Gaps in his memory like holes in Swiss cheese plagued him constantly. He felt that if he could get to his mother, maybe she could help fill the gaps and explain the violence aimed at Franklin Chase. Jason despaired of ever getting to her side. With the black Cadillac stalking the streets, he needed her more than ever.

The match struck and flared, pushing aside the darkness in the shed. Jason lit the candle he had brought from the house. "The library ladies are expecting me tomorrow after school," he said as he pulled the stool to the workbench and sat. "They have something for me to read." He paused. "You want to come along?"

"Can't." Suzy, her shoulder-length brown hair pulled from her face in a ponytail, watched the first drips of wax roll down the candle and freeze. "Me and Rachel have girl stuff to do. But tell Mary and Louise I said hi."

Mary Tremont and Louise Deloro had learned about Jason and his abilities a month earlier. After the mind modifications in late August, only Russ and Suzy knew his secret. Mary and Louise, who ran the town library, recognized Jason only as a talented, normal, young man willing to work hard to improve himself. They actively participated in that improvement.

Jason nodded. "What do you think about the car today?"

"You're sure it was them?" Suzy asked.

"No, not exactly. There was this mental squeeze." Jason rubbed his hands together, worried. "It's hard to explain." He paused, trying to recall the details. "It wasn't someone like me. There was no attempt to get inside my head."

"Then maybe it was someone like me," Suzy said. "You wouldn't have been able to read that mind either." She thought for a moment. "If you had tried to read him or her, you would have given yourself away. I know when you are trying to read my thoughts."

Jason agreed. Suzy was not like him, a telepath. She was something different.

"We need to keep an eye out for this black car." She put a hand on Jason's shoulder. "You're doing the right thing." She took a deep breath and released it slowly. "You knew they would show up sooner or later."

"Later would have been better." Jason caught Suzy's odd expression in the candlelight.

"I'm kinda curious," she said. "I would like to know what this person can do. I might learn something about me."

Jason looked at her, horrified. "Like what? Just walk up to him or her and ask? These people almost killed Patti!"

"Yeah, you're right. Direct contact would be a problem." With her fingertip she drew small circles on the benchtop.

Jason stared at her, surprised by her matter-of-fact attitude. "You don't seem all that worried."

"Jason, you made us invisible." She smiled at him. "You proved that today. I am sure that whoever drove that car would have come back around to check you out if they sensed anything." She rested her hand on his. He felt a pleasant shock and glanced her way and then watched the shadows dance on the wall over her shoulder.

"I'm just not sure we are 100 percent safe, ya know?" He watched Suzy pick a frozen piece of dripped wax from the stem of the candle. She held it in the flame and watched it melt.

"Let's see what Russ thinks," she said as she dropped the last of wax next to the wick. "Try not to worry too much until we have something to really worry about."

Jason suddenly noticed how grownup Suzy seemed.

"Tomorrow then," he said.

Suzy leaned forward and blew out the candle. Side by side they walked across the backyard to the house.

Chapter 2

The yellow taxi pulled to the curb. Lydia Dubois was abandoning her home, the old Victorian house, and its pathetic occupants. In a midnight-blue dress, high heels, and stylish hat, she hauled her heavy suitcase down the walk using both hands.

The driver jumped out and came around the front of the car. He relieved her of the heavy burden and then opened the trunk and hefted it in.

"Whew, got the kitchen sink in here?" he said with a smile. When he got no reaction from Lydia but a stare, he frowned and went around and opened the rear door for her. "What a head case," he mumbled to himself after closing the door. "A little makeup wouldn't hurt either." Once behind the wheel, he turned and asked, "Where to, lady?"

"The railway station." Lydia stared out of the window, her mind working her options. With twenty-five thousand dollars in cash in her suitcase, her loser of a brother would be happy to see her. They were cut from the same mold, shaped by the same family dynamics. There was never enough money.

Lydia, Jason's foster mother, failed to see the value of staying in the large house. In the year since Jason had arrived, she had cringed at every sign of improvement in the children in her care. The money stream from the prescription drugs, general upkeep, and special funds for seriously screwed-up foster kids had dried up. Then there was Frank. Her husband no longer cowered at her angry outbursts. He had showed unexpected strength when his mother died. Lydia cracked a smile, happy the desiccated old bird was dead. And love for her husband never played a part in her considerations.

The driver snatched looks at her in the mirror as he negotiated traffic. "Beautiful day, isn't it?" he said. Lydia did not react. He gave up trying to connect. It wasn't like he thought she was beautiful or anything. In fact, he thought her harsh with little saving grace.

Just drive, you idiot, she thought. Idiot? Lydia was not sure who was the bigger fool in this fiasco: Frank or her. Together they had gamed the foster care system raking in the excess dollars and selling unused pills for a decade. In a matter of months, the whole scam had crashed around her. Yet the State of Pennsylvania still considered them a good bet for the most difficult cases. The collapse of her gold mine remained unknown to the Department of Social Services. How it came about remained a mystery to her.

"A mystery," she said to the window. The boy, Jason—the toolshed kid—had defeated her schemes. How a thirteen-year-old had managed that feat escaped Lydia. She knew with certainty that Jason, who had lived for months in the backyard shed, had authored her downfall. She could not pound the memories loose in her head. Something about the boy teased and tortured her conscious mind. The key piece to the puzzle hovered inches out of her reach. Feeling the headache start, Lydia gave up.

Frank's newfound strength of character was another matter. His transformation made her remaining in the house impossible. Only a compliant, easily dominated slave would suffice for Lydia. With the toolshed boy entering the house, Frank changed like the kids. His compliance fell by the wayside.

No one had witnessed her strategic retreat, and she had left no note to explain her strange need. She chafed at the taxi's slow progress in the heavy traffic. Her foot never stopped tapping the floorboard.

The next day in the classroom, about the time Lydia folded and packed her clothes around the plastic-wrapped block of twenty-dollar bills, Jason realized that getting Russ's thoughts on the black car must wait until lunchtime. But first he had to tackle several surprise tests, covering history, math, and reading comprehension.

"I can't teach you if I don't know what you need." Mrs. Hatcher used that phrase repeatedly. She never explained how the results changed anything she did or how performance on the tests figured into a student's grade. Russ described her methods as terror tactics.

Jason devoured books of all sorts, so Mrs. Hatcher's tests did not challenge him. But they stressed Russ. Jason felt bad for his friend and helped him with the homework when asked. Artie never complained or asked for help. Since her two older misfits did well, Mrs. Hatcher focused her prejudices elsewhere for a while.

Reading over the first test, Jason randomly chose questions to answer incorrectly. A B grade was good enough. It kept Mrs. H off his back and raised no suspicions that he was anything other than a normal kid. The bell rang for lunch, and Jason with Russ in tow found Suzy waiting in the hallway. Russ tossed his lunchbox on the table in the lunchroom and collapsed into a chair.

"I think I failed the math test." He shook his head, looking forlorn. "Hatcher is a horror. She tests and then doesn't offer any help."

"When you talk to her, what does she say?" Suzy asked.

"Well, Mr. Wyatt." Russ sat up ramrod straight, put a fist on his hip, and glared, mimicking his teacher. "If you can't keep up, maybe we should find you an easier classroom."

"Oh," said Suzy, outraged, "how can they allow her to teach?"

"Yeah." Russ reached for his lunch box. "How? They do, though, because she's got seniority or something."

As Jason listened to their exchange, Russ glared at him from time to time, but Jason ignored him. He spread his peanut butter sandwiches and apple on the table. He had no interest in opening their discussion from a few days earlier. Russ figured Jason could solve his problem by making him smarter with a few mind changes. But Jason had refused his best friend's request, reminding him what a bad idea it was. "Even if there weren't dangerous people out there just waiting for me to use my power," Jason had said, "it's incredibly dangerous for you to have me messing around in your head. I mean, it's not like I have a map or instructions on what to do."

Jason unwrapped one of his sandwiches and took a bite.

When Suzy finished doing her best to cheer up Russ, he pulled his chair to the table. "So we are being tracked," he said as he opened his lunch box and pulled out a plastic-wrapped stack of cookies. He smiled weakly; homemade cookies made bad times a little less troubling.

"Something like that," Jason said with a mouthful of peanut butter. He drank chocolate milk from a small carton, which he had grabbed from the huge cooler at the entrance to the cafeteria.

"Jason thinks it's someone like me." Suzy looked at Russ. "We don't know what this person can do. It . . . sort of makes it scary to make any kind of move." Suzy grabbed her apple and crunched a big piece out of it.

"Suzy thinks you may have some ideas," Jason said to Russ, who was devouring his cookies slowly, one by one. At the last one, he paused and examined the chocolate chips pushing up through the brown-sugar surface.

"This person doesn't know what he or she has stumbled into," Jason said. "You need to know what he or she is doing."

Russ bit into the cookie like it might be the last one ever. He chewed with eyes closed, obviously appreciating the feel of chocolate on his tongue. "Set up lookouts; find out where this black car spends most of its time," he spoke softly. "You will learn what's interesting to this person and what's not."

Russ crumpled the wrapper, set it aside, and pulled out something wrapped in wax-paper. When he spread out the paper, two fried chicken legs lay there. The succulent aroma hung in the air. He grabbed one and took a big bite and then looked up at Jason. "So," continued Russ, chewing and using the drumstick as a pointer. He sounded like a professor stating the obvious for slow students. "If he sits in his car in front of your house, we know he has sensed something you did there."

"Yeah . . . or he may pick up what that dirtbag did to your sister and be at your house." Jason thought a moment. "I need to see if he hangs out someplace where the only possible reason is the mental stuff."

"Thas ma house," slurred Russ, his mouth full of fried chicken.

"Yeah, or the hospital in Kearny." Jason finished his sandwich thinking of Sally Tilghman, who had magically recovered from Alzheimer's disease there. "Nothing ever happened at the library. So my house or yours is the best bet."

Artie had been searching for a welcoming table when he saw Jason. "Can I join you?"

"Sure," the three of them said at the same time. Artie smiled.

"I'm kinda tired of eating alone." He sat and looked around the table. "The list will be out this afternoon." Like the others, he spread his lunch out on the table and began to eat.

"The list?" asked Russ.

"Yeah, who made the team . . . who didn't." Artie turned to Jason.

"Oh." Jason was not optimistic.

"My dad agrees with your foster dad. We got a good shot, man." Artie looked again at Russ, Suzy, and Jason. "Did I interrupt something?"

The three looked at each other, not knowing what to say. They could not tell Artie about Jason's situation.

"Sort of," Jason said slowly. "It's something you shouldn't know. A family thing I can't talk about. These guys know"—Jason nodded to Russ and Suzy—"because we've been together a long time."

"I get it." Artie's smile never left his face. "It's like my mom." He looked around, leaned in, and whispered, "She doesn't want anyone to know about how my uncle, her brother, ya know"—he stopped to make sure his audience understood—"nearly got himself lynched in York County back in the fifties."

"What?" Russ said, clearly offended. "That doesn't happen up here."

"What doesn't happen up here?" Jason asked, glancing from one to the other.

"It does, man," Artie said, looking directly at Russ. He turned to Jason and said, "People getting hung because they got dark skin."

Jason turned to Russ. "Is this one of those under-a-rock things?" Russ nodded. People became frustrated with Jason when he did not know the simplest of things. His mind had been reset, his memories cleared. The medication forced on him due the misdiagnosis made it worse. He missed out on a lot, though he was slowly reclaiming what he missed.

"Okay, fill me in." Jason waited, expecting a quick tutorial on what Artie was talking about. Russ said nothing. Jason turned to Suzy.

"People got killed, Jason . . ." She paused. "I think we should talk about this later."

"But . . . we're the north," insisted Russ.

"Happens everywhere, man," said Artie. "Happens everywhere."

"I guess," said Jason. "I need to read up on it."

The bell rang.

☆   ☆   ☆

"Niels Bohr, young man! A name you need to remember," insisted Mary Tremont as she leaned over the library front desk. Gray haired and heavyset, Mary was like a gruff but affectionate aunt you can count on. "He experimented with basic atomic structure: the hydrogen atom. It's all here." She handed Jason a thick, leather-bound book. "I think this may help with your questions on chemical bonding."

"Thank you, Mrs. Tremont. This is great." Jason flipped a few pages and scanned a few lines. His smile drooped. "How long can I keep it?"

She smiled. "Yes, it needs some study." She slapped the tabletop. "Just keep it as long as you need to." Her eyes focused on something over the Jason's right shoulder, and he followed her gaze. A dark-haired man looked up from his reading in a chair Jason practically lived. He had a large, purplish nose and a smile revealing crooked teeth.

"Sorry, Mr. Newton," Mary called. The man nodded and returned to his reading.

Jason felt a sudden revulsion, as if he had seen a cockroach skitter across a floor in an otherwise spotless kitchen. He knew better than to use his abilities.

"Who is that guy?" he asked.

"We're not sure," said Louise Deloro, Mary's sister. She had just come from the staff room behind a long bench with books stacked along its length. Where her sister was heavyset, Louise was slender. Her intuition plus her quick, analytic mind made her formidable in her line of work.

"He came to the library for the first time about two weeks ago. He's employed by an elderly home-care outfit in Kearny. His reading interests lean toward nonfiction books about unsolved crimes of the century." She took a deep breath and let it out while staring at Mr. Newton. "I am not quite comfortable with this person. Mary?"

"Gives me the creeps." Mary shook her head. "He's quiet enough and pleasant, but . . ."

Jason ignored his own revulsion. "How do you know where he works?"

"Because, young man, I look out the window from time to time." She feigned exasperation. "See the white van out front?"

"No." Jason tucked his new book under his arm.

"Well," Louise said, annoyed, "Mr. Newton has arrived several times over the last weeks in that van." She folded her arms and said, "If you care to check the writing on the vehicle, you will know what I know." Jason nodded and mumbled an apology.

All three turned as Mr. Newton got up abruptly. He abandoned his book on the cushion, where his posterior had left an impression. He left the library without a word. When the doors closed behind him, they all felt lighter, as though a burden had been lifted from their shoulders.

"Some tea before you go?" Mary turned to the staff room door without waiting for an answer.

"Will there be cookies?" Jason called.

"Of course," said Louise as she followed her sister.

The three spent the next hour drinking tea and eating cookies, discussing Jason's schoolwork and how to gain him entrance to a good college.

✻   ✻   ✻

The white van with "SeniorHomeAid" painted on its sides in large, black, Gothic letters rolled to a halt in front of a ranch-style home in Kearny, Pennsylvania. Mortimer Newton—Mort to his coworkers—killed the engine but left the radio on. He hummed the melody to the haunting organ opening in Bach's *Toccata and Fugue*. With the van windows down, a cool breeze blew across the front seat. Taking a deep breath, Mort watched the trees lining the street wave lazily. In a month or so, the dark green leaves would give way to the reds and golds of autumn. That was Mort's best time of year, just as the color changed and the dying began.

Leaning toward the empty passenger seat, Mort picked up his clipboard. He tapped a pencil in time with the counterpoint of Bach's masterpiece and hummed some of the notes climbing to heaven. He looked over his list. One client remained. He checked his watch, one in the afternoon on the dot. He smiled. His day would end ahead of schedule.

Mrs. Schlesinger, his morning appointment, he finished early. He spent his lunch hour in the Franklin Chase library, and now it was Mrs. Marjorie Rump's turn. Tossing the clipboard back onto the passenger seat, he opened the glove compartment and extracted a four-inch square mirror. He explored his reflection carefully.

"Perfect." He smiled. Not a strand of black hair was out of place, no imperfections on his pleasant face. His nose had just the right amount of purplish color to advertise his fight with the bottle. Many of the women he serviced, the conscious ones anyway, liked that he struggled with human weakness and won.

"They're all such mothers," Mort whispered, examining the blue eyes that stared back at him. Satisfied, he put the mirror back where he found it, pulled the keys out of the ignition, and tossed them into the opened attaché case lying on the van floor between the front seats. He sat a moment and then clapped his hands once. "It's showtime!"

Mort bounced out of the van, slammed the door behind him, and hurried to the back. Throwing open the rear door, he hauled out a case twice the size of his attaché. In it the SeniorHomeAid technician had all that he needed to do his job.

Mort charged up the walkway to the front door, rummaging in his pocket for the front-door key. His sky-blue, freshly washed and pressed coveralls swished as he walked. He found the chain of keys in his top left pocket, where the company logo was stitched. He inserted a key in the lock and turned it, but the door swung inward by itself. Mort watched the keys, torn from his grasp, dangle on the handle. Surprised, he looked up into the no-nonsense face of Amanda Rice.

"Mortimer." Amanda ran the show at SeniorHomeAid, and she never used nicknames. The team of techies who took pride in their "call" names found her insistence on calling them by their given names an affront. They put up with it out of respect for her incredible competence.

"We need to discuss Mrs. Rump's disposition. Grab your keys and come in." He watched her walk away in her nurse's uniform, thinking she might be attractive if she could stop the drill-sergeant routine. For a forty-something woman, she looked good from behind.

Mort reached for the keys and froze. Amanda injected herself into a client's care for only one reason. He or she died or was close to death and needed to be in the hospital or hospice.

"Mortimer! Don't dillydally." Her voice came from the back of the house where, Mort knew, Marjorie lay bedridden.

Mort grabbed the keys and clamored up the steps. He left the door opened and dropped the case he carried in the hall. As he entered the bedroom, the usual smells of urine and feces accosted him. An intravenous bottle fed fluids into Mrs. Rump's arm. This was new. Amanda, trained as a registered nurse, stood on the other side of the bed, holding the old woman's wrist, checking her pulse.

"Mortimer, you have done well keeping Marjorie in pretty good shape." She closed her eyes and paused, listening carefully. "The night person reported a significant decline at about midnight. I figured I would check in this morning." She paused again and pulled an errant strand of brown hair back behind her ear. "She has to go into the hospital now. She's close to death." Amanda never considered that this might upset Mort, who had worked hard with Mrs. Rump, as he did with all of his clients. "I have arranged for the move, but it will not happen until after three this afternoon. Damned hospitals." She laid Mrs. Rump's hand gently on the bed. "Can you stay with her until the ambulance arrives?"

"Of course," Mort said, staring at the unconscious woman. This would be their last time together. He shook his head disappointed; he had planned for at least two more visits. He couldn't believe it—two final meetings in the same day: Mrs. Schlesinger and now this.

"Good man." Amanda headed for the doorway. "Clean her up. I had another client to see an hour ago. I will leave her in your capable hands." In seconds, she was gone.

When Mort heard the engine of her car come to life, he relaxed. He never thought to look for a strange car on the street and made a mental note to correct his process.

"Well, Marjorie, it would appear that my timing is off a bit. Excuse me for a second." Mort left the room and picked up his case near the front door. He returned and set it on the dresser in the corner. Flipping the latches and raising the lid, he took out a pair of white cotton gloves and put them on. Over them he pulled rubber ones. He removed a syringe from the case and set it down on the dresser. Leaving the room a second time, Mort went to the kitchen, where he turned on Mrs. Rump's radio. Beethoven's *Midnight Sonata* filled the whole house.

"Nice," said Mort, appreciating the beauty of the music. "Very nice."

He returned to the bedroom. Gently, he moved her body to clean her waste and change the soiled sheets beneath her emaciated body. He sprayed the room and the whole house, room by room, with pine-scented air freshener.

"Now, Marjorie," he said, returning to her bedside, getting excited, "we have been together a long time." He went back to the dresser and picked up the syringe. He turned around and gazed at the skeletal woman on the bed. "And thank you, Nurse Rice," he whispered. His job was so much easier with the IV in place.

Mort stepped forward, watching the drip of the solution from the bottle to the tube. He grasped the line feeding Marjorie fluids and pushed the needle through the feeder connection. He paused and closed his eyes.

"We almost missed our rendezvous, Marjorie." Mort began to bounce up and down on the balls of his feet. "So many weeks of effort almost wasted. But we're together now, aren't we?" He applied pressure to the plunger of the syringe. His head fell back and his mouth hung open. Mort's whole body shuddered. In the calm that followed, he controlled himself and watched for Marjorie's body to react. It did not take long.

The old woman's eyes suddenly opened wide. She reached out for the bed railings and tried to sit up. Her eyes focused on Mort. There was an instant of recognition.

"My mom hated surprises," Mort said. He leaned over the bed railing and looked into her startled eyes. "Surprise!"

Marjorie fell back on the bed, unable to support herself, since her heart had given out and the blood no longer fed her brain. The last thing she saw was her caretaker's delighted smile.

Chapter 3

"Listen, Nurse Rice," said barrel-chested Detective Richard Cramer. "Mrs. Schlesinger and Mrs. Rump were old and going to die. Maybe that day, maybe in a week." He flipped his notebook closed with a "nobody cares" finality and stuffed it in a pocket in his tweed sports coat. "You say it was too soon. The doctor's say they were surprised they lasted as long as they did." He raised his arm and wagged his finger, shaking his head slowly in disbelief. "I've got nothing to say that a crime was committed. You're the only one with a complaint."

"I know. I know." Amanda bristled at the detective's dismissive, condescending attitude. "But I have never been wrong," she stated forcefully. "They passed too soon. How?"

"Listen, honey," Cramer said, "your say-so isn't enough to start a murder investigation for these old gals, who would've been dead anyway. One week early, one week late?" He shrugged, implying clearly as that it didn't matter. He considered this whole episode a waste of time.

Amanda growled on the inside. *Stupid man,* she thought.

"What about Mort Newton?" she said. "Where is he? Why was the van found abandoned by the lake?" She crossed her arms and dug her nails into her upper arms, trying to control her rage. Better to control herself than have a criminal record for assaulting a cop.

"Well," said Cramer, "as far as we can tell, Mr. Newton is missing, and we will follow up. Of course," he said with a sigh and a fatherly, condescending tone, "his coworkers said this happens from time to time to the technicians who work hard with these patients. They think Mort lost it and bailed."

Amanda could not argue. A significant part of her job involved replacing burned-out men and women who became attached to their patients and hit an emotional bottom when their charges died.

"Or . . . he might be dead. Murdered by the same nutcase," she said.

"When we have evidence, Miss Rice, we will pursue it." Cramer turned abruptly and headed to his car. "You're the nutcase," he muttered as he walked away.

Amanda caught it. "It is not for us to decide the value of living a day, a week . . ." she yelled to the detective's back. He waved her off.

Amanda sat at her desk. The fingers of her left hand lightly touched her forehead while her right scribbled furiously. Amanda, the lead medical professional for SeniorHomeAid, would not be ignored. Something very bad had been happening among her elderly charges. She knew it. She felt it in her bones but could not prove it.

"Stupid cop." The pencil tip snapped, and she tossed it. It bounced around in the green, metal trash can; the sharp banging measured the level of her frustration. She pulled another pencil from her large, brown saddle-bag purse. Once finished with the letter to her boss, she grabbed her dog-eared notebook and opened it to a specific page. Her pencil tapped the page as her eyes wandered to a yellowing, grocery tabloid lying next to her bag. Her heart cooled. This was not fair or acceptable.

"Why you, Sally Tilghman?" she said aloud. Amanda studied the picture of Sally, who had miraculously recovered from Alzheimer's disease, but she discounted the fuzzy one of the boy. "Why did you deserve this second chance?"

Amanda shook her head, stepped back from a pit of depression, and chided herself. It did not matter. Instantly, she was tossed back in time. She remembered how the doctors back from the war had forced her out of her medical kingdom at the Veteran's Hospital. From late 1943 to the end of the war, she had diagnosed, prescribed, treated, and taken care of wounded soldiers. She was good.

Her days in the wards of the wounded boys passed in a blur. Sometimes fourteen hours at her post or in emergency situations, Amanda stole an hour's sleep when she could. She saved lives. In all but name, she was a doctor.

It came to an abrupt end with the war's end. With the male doctors returning, her role collapsed to basic nursing. She found herself correcting incoming interns, who resented a woman trying to tell them how to do their jobs. The University of Louisville offered Amanda a place in the medical school based on the recommendations from the doctors who had monitored her work during the war years. She needed a few college courses to get in. Amanda heard that two women had made it through and graduated. Money, she rationalized, held her back. In truth she bridled at the need to prove herself again to the men who controlled the gates. Furious and fed up, Amanda quit the VA. She was thirty.

A horn blast startled Amanda back to the present. The SeniorHomeAid van passed the front of the office. Solomon Freeman had announced his return. She looked at her watch. Her efforts were needed elsewhere. Without thinking, Amanda had moved her appointment with Sally to that afternoon. She closed her books and packed them away. Rising and pulling the strap over her shoulder, she grabbed the tabloid, folded it, and stuffed it under her arm.

"Stop whining and get out there."

☆   ☆   ☆

Mortimer Newton ceased to exist when the last vestiges of the makeup were removed from his face. The van sat abandoned by Lake Quinatoab, scrubbed of all evidence. After finishing with the SeniorHomeAid van, Mort—now Mr. Smith—walked to the railway station parking lot where he picked up his car, a gray Impala, just after dark. He hit a number of local bars in and around Kearny. By midnight, false ID cards lay in several bars, restaurants, and grocery-store dumpsters in the town.

Looking at himself in the bathroom mirror in a local, cheap motel, he wondered who to be this time. This would be his last effort in Pennsylvania. One more play, he thought, before moving on.

"Maryland, perhaps." He smiled at his reflection and then scanned the dresser top. Four stacks of identity cards lay neatly side by side. On the motel registry he was Mr. Gerald Smith.

"Who to be, who to be," he said in a soft, singsong voice.

"Chet Winston, I think." Mr. Smith smiled, picked up the driver's license, and studied it intently. Unlike Mortimer, playing the part of Chet required no makeup. Mr. Smith could be himself. He laughed at the thought. He had not been himself for ten years, since the fire consumed the house and his sleeping family. Somehow all the escape routes were blocked, and the flames moved fast along a well-laid trail of charcoal lighter fluid.

"They weren't all that nice anyway." Mr. Smith addressed his reflection in the mirror. He rubbed his face with his right hand; he felt the stubble on his neck and along his jawline. The beginnings of a shadow on his cheeks bothered him. "Unacceptable," he said. "Cut you down, I will." He would use the safety razor until he bled. Only smooth skin would do.

Shaved and clean, Mr. Smith realized he was incredibly hungry. He wiped the drops of blood off the sink with a tissue as the pink water drained away. Dressed, he gathered the paper and folded it neatly. Intent on a late-morning breakfast at the nearest diner, Smith tapped the paper on his opened hand. He looked forward to examining the want ads over strong coffee.

✶   ✶   ✶

"C'mon," Frank insisted. "I need some company, and you're the only one up."

Jason stared at his foster father from his bed. The leather-bound book lay open, propped up on his thighs. He looked over at the clock on his desk. It was seven-thirty in the morning. "Where to?" he asked.

"I have to deal with some stuff at the hospital that belonged to my mother." Frank whispered the last few words. He coughed and wiped his eye. "I'll drop you at school on the way back and sign you in as unavoidably late."

"Yeah, give me a minute." Jason felt bad about Frank's mother's death. He would do anything to help him deal with the issue. He had made their last days of reconciliation possible. Edna, Frank's mother, considered her son to be pond scum. With a bit of telepathic effort, the truth blazed before her. She could not ignore it and cried out for her son, overwhelmed by her rediscovered feelings. Four days later she suffered a cerebral hemorrhage due to uncontrolled, high blood pressure.

Frank grinned. "Great! We'll have a late breakfast at the local diner." He turned and headed down the hall with a spring in his step. "Ten minutes and we are on the road!"

Forty minutes later, Jason and Frank hauled the first cardboard boxes of Edna's effects from the storage room at the State Hospital. By nine-thirty, they had collected everything Edna had left behind, so they headed for breakfast.

"I can't wait to go through some of that stuff," Frank said, excited to learn more about the mother who had abandoned him long ago.

Jason might have saved her life if he knew about her condition. He did not do a thorough job, and Edna died quietly in her sleep on the fifth day. Jason was determined not to make that mistake again.

The ride to the diner was quiet. Jason figured Frank was reliving those days as he drove. Memories of the old, emaciated Sally Tilghman, tied to a wheelchair, passed through Jason's mind. For no clear reason, she had struggled to roll close to him that day when Frank dragged a few of the Dubois kids to the hospital. She had grabbed his hand. Instantly, the damaged corridors of her brain had appeared in Jason's mind. He had done what he could; it had been enough to counter the dementia. His picture with Sally on the front cover of the tabloid had caused him no end of trouble with people seeking miracles for loved ones.

Frank and Jason pushed through the glass doors of the diner and took a booth at the far end of the restaurant.

"The coffee here is very good," Frank said as they settled into the booth. He looked at Jason expectantly. "It'll definitely get you through the day."

Two cups appeared on the table with milk and sugar. Frank ticked off the pluses and minuses of sugar and milk in coffee. Jason sipped the coffee black. It was awful. He experimented with the additives. When satisfied, he raised his mug. Frank did the same, and they toasted nothing in particular.

Jason was surprised by the changes in Frank since he had joined the household. Every parenting skill he lacked with Lydia in control came roaring back and erupted, bringing hope to a dark, hopeless house. When he took the younger kids out front and started tossing the football around before school started, Jason joined in the fun. It was Frank who said that Jason had talent and that if he wanted to play for the middle school team he would be happy to show him a few things.

"It won't be easy," Frank had said, throwing a bullet pass that Jason caught on his fingertips. "You need to get stronger."

"Let's do it, Frank." Jason had felt jubilant; he had a chance to be a normal kid.

Jason felt the rush as the caffeine hit his system. Then a sudden sense of revulsion struck him. It was familiar. He looked around, expecting to see Mr. Newton, but only one other person was in the diner, sitting in a booth at the other end of the diner. He looked nothing like the man from the library. Jason ignored the feeling and agreed with something Frank said about Coach Gunther.

"Let's order." Frank flipped open the menu.

The coffee at Rube's Diner near the State Hospital was strong. Mr. Smith, now trying on his Chet Winston identity, had arrived at the greasy spoon after ten. The breakfast crowd had dwindled; the diner was empty. Chet had taken a booth at the opposite end of the diner and spread out the newspaper. Quickly he checked the want ads for guy and gal Fridays.

"What's it going to be, hon?" asked the gum-chewing waitress. He thought she looked silly in the pink gingham dress. She turned when two new patrons entered the diner. The two men, one older and the other a teenager, took a booth at the diner's far end. She returned her attention to her immediate customer.

"Two eggs over medium, sausage, potatoes, and more coffee." Chet never looked up; he concentrated on the paper.

"You want white toast?" The waitress scribbled on her pad and then stopped, waiting for his final confirmation. Chet looked up from his paper into dull brown eyes.

She reached into her apron pocket and offered him a bunch of napkins. "Shaved a bit too close?" She brought the napkins up under her chin and pantomimed wiping it away.

"Rye toast." He stared at her as he took the napkins and pressed them under his jaw. She started to turn away. "Excuse me, but have we met before?"

Turning back, she studied his features and then said, "No. I don't think so."

"My mistake, sorry. You looked familiar." Chet smiled.

"I get that a lot." She stayed a moment, expecting more. When Chet remained silent, she turned away and headed to the kitchen.

He examined the columns of ads, smiling. *Mort,* he thought, *is truly gone.* He and associates from SeniorHomeAid had eaten in this diner often. He knew the waitress could not identify him.

The want ads held nothing new. The SeniorHomeAid ad was a mainstay in the help-wanted section. He ignored it. Giving up on the day's opportunities, he perused the "local" section. The article about the return of a Mrs. Tilghman caught his attention. He read with great interest how the woman had gained a reprieve from a disease that stole memories, self-awareness, and life.

"What so special about you, Sally Tilghman?" Chet read and was further shocked to find that she was a SeniorHomeAid client. *This is not fair in any way,* he thought. His outrage rose. Was she something special? Did a merciful God choose her for some heavenly reason?

"I think not." Chet fumed. "I am God's tool to bring justice and fairness." Rectification was needed. He drummed his fingers on the table. Should he or shouldn't he?

"Here ya go, hon." The waitress stood at the table, balancing two plates and a fresh pot of coffee. "Eggs over medium, sausage, potatoes, and rye toast." She smiled and placed the plates in front of Chet as he pushed the paper aside. "Anything else?" Her smile looked tired.

"No, thank you." Chet's excitement grew. He never hesitated when fate tossed a gem at his feet. Well fed, he would present himself for hiring at SeniorHomeAid.

"This was meant to be." He dug into his breakfast and enjoyed every bite.

Chapter 4

In his hotel room, Bill Sorenson dialed his home phone in Bismarck, North Dakota. There were a number of clicks, and then he heard the regular ringtone. After three, the phone was answered.

"Hello." Reena's voice was music to his ears.

"It's me," Bill said. Without thinking, his hand slid back and forth over the blanket.

"Miss you . . ."

"I know." Bill longed for her. He held the receiver with both hands.

"Tell me what you have." Reena wanted to keep the call focused.

"The girl lives." Bill described what he had observed. His wife did not interrupt his report. "What do you want me to do?"

"Stay," she said. "Maintain your observations. I suspect it may be a matter of time before we can be sure we have covered all the possibilities."

"I keep thinking of you," Bill said.

"I know." Reena paused. "You know what we want to do."

"Avoid war." Bill stood and put his hand in his pocket.

"Yes," she said. "At all costs."

"Understood." Even when separated by thousands of miles, he felt the tug.

"I want you." Reena's voice echoed his desire. After a long silence, she sighed. "Help us to be sure."

"I will." He hung up the phone. The longer he remained away from her, the harder it was not to rush home at the sound of her voice. But he never wanted to experience such violence among those of his kind again. Whole communities had ceased to exist. He had been a search-and-destroy enforcer. Bill found them; his fellow soldiers, like Rodney, destroyed them.

Searching exhausted him. He fell asleep with Reena's smile nudging him into sweet oblivion, and he napped the rest of the afternoon.

☆   ☆   ☆

"Hello? SeniorHomeAid calling," shouted Amanda. She entered the client's home, removed her jacket, and hung it in the closet by the front door.

"Amanda? Is that you?" a voice called from the back of the house.

"Yes, Sally. How are things going?" Amanda walked into the living room. The bright floral prints dominant on the furniture and curtains gave the room a homey feel. She smiled and looked around, happy to be back in a house she never expected to enter again.

Amanda set her bag down on the couch and headed for the kitchen. Sally Tilghman sat at the island, sipping coffee; a pair of dirty garden gloves lay on the counter. She wore a white T-shirt and overalls. Her eyes bright and full of life, she smiled, genuinely happy to see Amanda.

"Things are fine." Sally tilted her head to the ancient percolator on the gas stove. "Help yourself to coffee. I just made it." She noted that Amanda did not project her usual confidence and gung-ho spirit. Usually loud and energetic, the younger woman was subdued.

"Don't mind if I do." Amanda smiled as she pulled a white mug from the cupboard above the stove. The words "SeniorHomeAid" wrapped around the mug she pulled from the cupboard. The words "We take the time to care" caught her eye. She stopped and stared at the cup, wondering if those words were still true.

"Been working the weeds in your garden?" she asked, noting the gloves.

"More than weeds this year. I've planted a whole crop of salad fixings: lettuce, carrots, tomatoes, and celery." Sally, confined to a wheelchair for so long with no hope, sounded proud of her accomplishment. She would not waste any of the gift given: time. "Milk's in the fridge," she said.

Amanda, unused to questioning the social good of her employer, focused on the moment. "I'm a miner's daughter. I take it black." She filled the mug and parked in the chair next to Sally. She drank and sat back smiling. "This is a good cup of coffee." She turned to the older woman, gave her the once-over, and said, "You look good."

"You, on the other hand, look like a person with something on her mind." Sally smiled.

"Just work." She hoped the throwaway line would end it. Revealing herself or any loss of confidence to a client flew against her professionalism.

"Don't want to talk about it or don't want to talk about the deaths of other patients with another client?"

Amanda sat back. She froze, shocked, only able to stare at her hands and debate her next step. Someone needed to listen, and here was an open invitation. Amanda took a deep breath and turned to Sally. "How did you know?"

"I read the paper, you know." She frowned and shook her head. "Marjorie Schlesinger was a longtime friend of mine. We went to grammar school together. I was sorry to hear she died, but not surprised. She was eighty-six after all." She sipped her coffee and caught Amanda staring at her. "What?"

Angrier than she intended, Amanda shot at Sally, "You were not supposed to come back . . . to recover."

"Well." Sally paused. She thought of the young man she wanted so much to see again. "Maybe I was just touched by an angel." A smile grew and then fell. "Now, what has upset you so?"

Amanda forced a grin. She glanced out the window and watched a bird soar into and then out of the frame. She reached out and patted Sally's arm gently. "I don't need to burden you with my problems."

"I think . . ." Sally set her cup on the counter. "I am the perfect person to burden." She patted Amanda's arm in return and said, "Tell me. I think you have some of your own weeds to pull."

Amanda coughed as if clearing her throat. "Well . . . I have lost a number of clients recently. I mean, I expected it . . . but it all happened—"

"Too soon?" Sally kept her hand on the younger woman's arm. She wanted to keep in touch with Amanda, not the professional nurse. "Tell me," she whispered.

"They died when all the test results said 'not yet.'" A tear escaped Amanda's control and rolled off her cheek onto the counter. "No one cares. They were old and would die anyway." She shook her head, frustrated.

"So what do you think happened?" Sally stood up, went to the stove, picked up the coffee pot, and filled her cup. She returned to the island with the pot and filled Amanda's cup. "You suspect foul play?"

"Yes . . . no . . . I'm not sure." *Would a week or two really matter?* Amanda asked herself. "It's not like they had a life." She took a long drink of the hot coffee. "It just isn't right that they might have been sent on prematurely." She looked at Sally. "Do you know what I mean?"

Sally nodded. "There is someone you must meet. He is a child, but he may be able to help."

"A child." Amanda laughed, frustrated.

"Someone very special. Believe me. I know." Sally patted her arm. She walked over to a row of books on the counter near the range. Most were cookbooks; she pulled out the yellow phonebook. "Now, you want to go to Franklin Chase." She turned the directory around to face Amanda and kept her finger pointing at the number and address. "Bring him here, and we all can talk about it."

Amanda stared, unsure.

"Amanda," Sally insisted, "bring me my angel."

✣　　✣　　✣

Frank sat at the kitchen table, surveying the group of misfit kids who had become a family over the last few months. The older boys and girls cleared the dinner plates and then placed the two trays of brownies and milk containers on the table.

"Can't enjoy brownies without cold milk." Frank laughed as the children waited for his signal. He raised his hand, and said, "Please, everyone gets one, maybe two, if I've counted correctly."

Hands shot out, grabbing the chocolate squares until the trays and milk cartons were empty. Frank watched, gratified by the moment of joy. It was a small bit of pleasure for his charges. He nodded to Jason, who returned his recognition with a slight tilt of his head.

Frank and Jason shared a special relationship. Jason's knowhow on the football field came from Frank's coaching. Frank, once free of Lydia, had blossomed.

Jason took a brownie after the others had taken theirs. He thought it strange that only in the last few months had he taken the time to know more about the other children living in the Dubois house. Of course, there was Suzy, Rachel, and Sam. Lydia had tried to use Sam to manipulate Jason. It hadn't worked. After that episode, she started having headaches whenever she plotted to use people for nefarious purposes, because Jason had set traps in her mind.

"So." Frank patted the table nervously. "I have some announcements." He hesitated a moment and rubbed at an imagined spot on the table. "Okay." He looked up at the expectant faces, some with chocolate smiles. "Lydia is not in bed with one of her headaches. She's gone." No one reacted. "She may come back. She may not. I just don't know."

"Where'd she go?" asked Sam.

"Since she left no note, I'm not sure." He took off his glasses and wiped them on his shirt. "Things won't change very much around here with her gone." He replaced his glasses and smiled. "You guys have been doing great together. Nothing should change on that score. Okay?"

Heads around the table nodded. None knew how to react to Lydia's abandonment. Cautious relief started with Jim, the eldest boy in the house, and then a wave of smiles wrapped around the table. Bodies relaxed; supportive arms found their way around shoulders.

Jason broke off a piece of brownie and popped it in his mouth.

"The other bit of news is for the older kids. Some of you have been here long enough to know what happened to other kids that aged out of the social services programs. We let them go." Frank stopped. He frowned, took a deep breath, and said, "No, we abandoned them to the street." He hesitated. "I'm not proud of that, and it's time to fix these mistakes."

Looking at Jim, Frank continued, "When you turn eighteen, you don't have to leave until you have someplace to go."

Jim turned to Sylvia, who would turn eighteen two months after he did. He could tell she was near tears with relief. Her only recourse would have been to return home. She made up her mind never to return to that war zone.

"Thank you," Sylvia said. Afraid, she asked, "How long can we stay?"

"Well, Sylvia, as long as it takes to get you on your feet." Frank considered his next words. "I think you need to work a job for a while. Get comfortable with taking care of yourself." He paused and then became aware of the silence. "I will have to find some opportunities where you can start."

Jim was not convinced by this turnabout. "You mean you are going to help us even though there's no money in it?"

"Yes." Frank held his gaze. "You start at the Ford dealership next week. Just a short stint to see if you like the auto business. The library downtown needs some part-time help too." He turned to Sylvia. "I thought that would be a good place to start for you, Sylvia. Mrs. Deloro said she could use the help."

They all sat in silence. Was this a dirty trick?

Frank continued. "This is how it will go for all of you. No one gets left behind or tossed to the street. Everyone will leave here with a path to get on with life." Frank understood their doubt. "Actions speak louder than words, so you will have to be patient and see how it goes with Jim and Sylvia." Eyes stared at Frank, not knowing what to say. A few heads nodded. "Okay!" Frank clapped his hands. "Who is up for a long game of Monopoly?" Hands shot up on all sides of the table. "That's the spirit!"

Jason sat dumbfounded. A sudden chill ran up his spine. He realized Frank's new attitude came from him. Was this house a glowing target of psychic energy?

Chapter 5

Reena Sorenson sat at her kitchen table, lost in thought. She wanted Bill home and she knew something must be done with Rodney, the Northeast Community leader. Her hands wrapped around a coffee cup; it was cold. She frowned then concentrated; the coffee steamed. The spoon sitting next to the sugar bowl levitated then sank into the hot cup and stirred the settled sugar.

Rodney's malfeasance was painfully obvious. The girl lived. Far worse, the girl may have been a normal person, a "norman" in the vulgar use of the word.

"A norman." Reena chuckled, sipping her coffee. People without Community talents were called normals. Over time, the more base description came into ready use.

It rolls so easily off the tongue, she thought. Placing the cup on the table, she became all business. Rodney must go, his power stripped and his life drained of all knowledge of the Community. *Yes, an extraction.*

Reena needed a popular yet talented puppet to take his place. She promptly stood, went to the wall phone, and dialed.

"Samantha, dear."

"Reen-na?" a voice stuttered.

"Rodney will be extracted." Reena did not require a response. "You will take his place." She waited a few heartbeats. "You understand?"

"Yes." There was no hesitation, no room for debate.

"Good." Reena hung up the phone.

"Mr. Sutter!" The name echoed down the hallway and commanded immediate attention.

Like everyone else in the hallway, Jason froze, just as he reached into his locker for a textbook. Slowly heads turned in his direction. He and Artie made the unwritten list of students everyone in the school recognized. They were the only two seventh-graders in school history to make the football team.

"A word, if you will!" The collective release of pent-up breath and stressed muscles pushed time back into its normal flow. Movement restarted, locker doors slammed, and spontaneous laughter erupted. Jason smiled.

Mr. Kyle Downing descended on Jason as he pulled his book from the locker, closed the door, and faced his old substitute teacher and friend.

"I have something for you," said Downing. He reached into his jacket's inside pocket. His other arm went across Jason's shoulders, and he gathered him to his side. Downing held up an ivory envelope and slid it between the pages of the textbook Jason held. "An invitation," he whispered.

"No!" Jason almost laughed.

"Long overdue, my boy, long overdue." Downing removed his arm from Jason's shoulders and walked with him down the hall. "Your fault really, dragging me down to the library at all hours." He paused and then chuckled. "I believe Mary and I are in your debt for bringing us close enough to recall the attraction."

A few months earlier, Downing and Mary, with her sister, Louise, were friends and confidants, fully aware of Jason's psychic gifts. Downing and Chiang Chen, who had experienced the ravages of war firsthand, guessed that there had been some kind of conflict among groups of people like Jason. In their view, the wrong side won. Some kind of dictatorship existed, stamping out all opposition or potential opposition. With Mary and Louise, they joined the circle of friends that enabled Jason to modify many memories. During this time, Downing and Mary had been thrown together while trying to help this teenage psychic phenomenon.

Just before school started, Jason rearranged their knowledge of him. He needed to hide. The clues wiped from the surface of their minds guaranteed another like him could not discover his existence. Now, Downing, Mary, and Louise, the teacher, and the library researchers believed they conspired to get him into college as early as possible. Jason became Downing's unofficial favorite student with support from Mary and Louise.

This struck Jason at the time as the best way to play the situation. They would not betray him with an errant thought, nor would they be in any danger of harm as conspirators against some very powerful people—the people who almost murdered Russ's sister.

"So," said Downing, "bring along that delightful friend of yours, Suzy. I think Russell should also join us, if it is approved by his parents."

"Yes, sir," said Jason. "I appreciate your inviting me."

"Nonsense, my boy." Downing stopped, and Jason turned to face him. "You had a hand in my recovery when I had that episode over the summer." He smiled and started walking down the hall again.

Downing did not know that Jason had caused the episode. In Downing's basement, while Jason was using a brass microscope, his inner sight had kicked in. When Downing touched Jason's neck with his bare hand, he had shot down the rabbit hole on a roller-coaster ride on rails of organic molecules. Downing had collapsed from the experience but no longer had access to the memory.

"Besides, Mary insists," Downing said. "She finds your talents interesting and your goal most laudable." Jason left them with the knowledge of his love of books.

As they neared the end of the hall, Jason saw Mrs. Hatcher staring. Impatient, she stood in the doorway of the classroom; she could not interrupt a fellow teacher with greater seniority.

"I better get to class." Jason put his hand on Downing's shoulder and said, "Thanks. We'll be there."

"She's been checking your records and the Negro boy's," said Downing in a barely audible voice. "Watch your back. Let your friend know." He nodded and nudged Jason forward. "Better not to be late," he said louder for Mrs. Hatcher's benefit.

"Me too?" Russ asked. Suzy, Jason, and Russ were at the toolshed after school.

"That's what he said," Jason replied, sitting comfortably on his stool leaning on the tool bench. "Your parents going to let you go?"

"Sure. Why not?" Russ shrugged. "The wedding isn't until December anyway. I mean, how long do ya need to plan for something?"

"Will Frank let us go?" asked Suzy. Strands of glossy brown hair escaped the rubber band holding back her ponytail; it fell lazily across her cheek. Jason felt something, a pull, when his eyes followed the flow of her hair across her face.

He pushed the feeling for Suzy aside. "Like Russ said, it won't happen until December. He's okay with it." He turned to Russ and asked, "Any news on the black car?"

"Oh, yeah, I almost forgot." Russ knocked his forehead as if freeing stuck thoughts. "The black car's been hanging in our neighborhood but closer to my house than yours. In fact, the guy in the car might've been at my front door."

"How do you know that?" Suzy asked, shocked.

"'Cause I got friends all over, and they told me." He paused for emphasis. "They saw the car in front of my place, and then the same guy passed out behind the wheel over on Henshaw Street. That's closer to my place than yours." Russ sat back satisfied.

"He wasn't passed out." Jason turned to Suzy. "He was doing something. Maybe seeing something with his mind." With his focus on Suzy, he spoke to Russ. "This is good news. He sees your place but not Frank's. He doesn't know about me."

"Yeah, unless he sees Patti, ya know?" Russ looked worried.

"He can't." Jason focused on Russ. "If he could he wouldn't still be looking. Besides, I hid her well." Jason returned his attention to Suzy. "We need to know what he might be doing to check things out. I just don't know how we will figure that out."

They sat in silence. The wind picked up. Yellow, red, and brown leaves rustled in the oak's branches and tumbled along the ground.

"You showed us what you do when you meditate," Suzy said. "Chiang taught Russ and me how." She paused. "But we"—she pointed to Jason and then herself—"never did it together. Maybe we should try . . . that . . . together. We might learn something." Suzy no sooner uttered the words than she felt very embarrassed. *What is this all about?* She rubbed her face, trying to wipe away her shyness and confusion. "I don't know. Just an idea, ya know?"

"A darn good one," said Russ, who had watched Jason protect Patti and control people's thoughts from a meditative state. "Jason, you've said Suzy is one of you. This might open a door or two to find how she fits in. Might make sure my sister stays safe."

"Worth a try," Jason said. "I wonder though if we are giving something away if we meditate. Will it show them where to find us?"

"When was the last time you joined Chiang in a session?" asked Russ.

"Not since we were all together at the end of the summer." Jason felt bad that he'd lost contact with his Chinese friend over the last months. Chiang Chen, Kyle Downing, had known about Jason but now only thought of him as a bright, talented, normal kid.

"Well, ya gotta try something," Russ insisted.

"Okay." Jason looked around the shed. "Let's sit on either end of the cot, facing each other with our legs crossed as Chiang taught us." Jason got off the stool. "Russ, you be our lookout." Suzy did not move.

"What do I look for?" Russ asked. "I mean . . . it's not like lights are going to turn on or anything."

Jason considered this as he held out his hand to Suzy. "Just observe what happens, okay?"

"Got it." Russ saluted and turned around on his stool to face the cot.

"I guess since this guy's not been near here, we won't be setting off any signal flares," Jason said. His hand still outstretched, he waited patiently for the feel of Suzy's hand in his.

Slowly, Suzy's hand grasped Jason's. She slid off the stool. She and Jason took their positions and started the process of clearing their minds.

Russ watched them intently: one for a moment, then the other. He did this for thirty minutes. His report afterward noted that they both hovered a few inches above the cot. Russ was not surprised by this strange levitation; whenever Jason meditated, he floated. Russ considered it pretty cool. Afterward, neither Jason nor Suzy could look the other in the face. No words escaped their lips.

"Well," asked Russ, annoyed by their silence, "did you find out anything or not?"

"No!" said Suzy and Jason at the same time.

Russ stared at them, confused.

✲   ✲   ✲

"When will your references get to us?" Amanda Rice had received a call from her boss. Since she requested help with hiring, she could not complain that a new applicant, who met with his approval, sat across from her at her desk. Although Mr. Winston looked capable, Amanda did not like putting someone in a client's home without confirmation of his previous experience, plus some character references. Placing a wolf among the ailing and weak sheep would be disastrous.

"I sent the request a week ago to the Maine headquarters," he said. "I expect to receive their note in a week or so. If you want to wait, that would be fine." Chet knew that SeniorHomeAid was barely keeping up with their clients' needs. He had gambled that they would not wait to put him to work. His plan called for no more than a few weeks to locate his target, dispatch her, and then move on to more fertile ground. The longing to correct God's indiscriminant injustice, to realign the universe on its purposeful path, drove Chet to distraction.

"We can use you, Mr. Winston," Amanda said.

"I'm sorry," he said, "I was momentarily distracted. You were saying?"

"I was saying," Amanda began as she studied her new employee carefully, shocked that he would say such a thing to her, "I have a few semiambulatory clients, men, who could use your services immediately. So you can start tomorrow. Meet me here at eight tomorrow morning, and I will take you around to meet these clients." Amanda closed the file containing her boss's assessment.

Chet spoke with a slight southern lilt. When Amanda first met him, she thought there was something familiar about Mr. Winston. She did not have time to analyze her impression or Mr. Winston's quirks.

Chet stood and shook her hand. "I'll be here," he said. "I am looking forward to getting started." He left the office, grinning ear to ear. It would not take long to locate Sally Tilghman; he shivered ever so slightly at the prospect.

Chapter 6

The first game of the junior high school season started at noon on Saturday October 3. The Hoover Jaguars took the field against the St. Augustine Eagles. St. Augustine was a Catholic high school near Philadelphia run by the Christian Brothers. Their junior varsity squad competed with the junior high public school teams.

The second quarter drew to an end. On the field, Artie and Jason lined up on the same side. The ball on the Eagle's twenty-five-yard line would go to Artie on a simple down-and-out pass pattern. Jason's job was to get the guy covering him to follow him to the middle of the field.

The ball snapped into the quarterback's hands. The linebackers blitzed. The quarterback, hit from two sides, fired the ball short to get rid of it. Jason, surprised but in the right place, reached low and snagged the ball on his fingertips. Pulling it into his gut, he dropped his head and shoulders as the bigger player grabbed air. Jason planted his left foot, changed direction on a dime, and charged up the field. The cornerbacks and safeties were all over Artie. Jason crossed into the end zone untouched. When the whistle blew ending the half, the Jaguars held a fourteen-point lead.

In the sparsely populated bleachers, Brother Joseph Michaels, St. Augustine's assistant principal, shook his head while stepping down to the field. It would be another season of the godless public-school squads running rings around the Catholic teams. It infuriated him. The coach's pep talk in the locker room fell flat. With the rival team fourteen points ahead, how could God be on St. Augustine's side? God smiled, it seemed, on the small-time, underfunded, secular team. They would win; those two receivers made amazing plays.

Fortunately, Brother Michaels had the mandate to bring promising candidates to St. Augustine. Usually, promising meant exceptional academic performance. He would stretch the meaning to include one of these two boys. He would have to move quickly to get them through the entrance exam. He was too late for this season. But he thought, *Get ready for next year!*

"Varsity," Brother Michaels spoke out loud as he walked the St. Augustine sideline. "No use pretending we don't need help."

Brother Michaels approached a large man whose tie flowed down the contours of his considerable stomach. "Coach?" The big man turned. "If you could pick a player from the opposing team to help out our struggling boys, whom would you pick?"

"Both."

The Jaguars won handily. Jason and Artie both caught touchdown passes in the second half. Coach Gunther slammed both boys on the shoulder pads, delighted with their performance. Even Logan, the middle linebacker, cornered them in the locker room and gave them credit for the victory. The boys played down the accolades. They were just happy the team won their first game.

Later that afternoon, back in his room, propped up against a pillow with his legs bent at the knees, giving him a place to rest an opened text, Jason relaxed. Success on the gridiron meant punished ribs. The soreness was tolerable if he did not move. Still trying to comprehend how molecules hung together, he ignored the loud slamming of the brass knocker on the front door. He heard Frank call out, "I'm coming. I'm coming." The door opened, and it got quiet.

Minutes passed. A sharp knock on his door was followed by his foster father's head.

"Hey, Jason."

"Frank?" Jason glanced up from his book. "What's up?"

"Someone to see you." Frank raised an eyebrow. *What didn't you tell me?*

"Oh?" Jason shrugged, signaling ignorance. "Who is it?"

"No one I know." Frank turned away and headed down the hallway. "Come and see for yourself," he called over his shoulder.

Jason slowly stretched out his legs and rolled off the bed, taking care to minimize the pain. He descended the stairs, not happy to give up his studies or his pain-free comfort. An attractive, older woman in nursing whites stood in the living room. She stared out the window.

"Miss Rice." Frank placed his hand on Jason's shoulder. "This is Jason Sutter."

"Jason," said Frank. "This is . . ."

"Amanda Rice, young man," she said, taking two confident steps and extending her hand.

"Yes," Frank said, flustered. Jason almost laughed as his foster dad was tossed into adolescent confusion. This was the first adult female to enter the house in a long time.

"May I speak to the boy alone, Mr. Dubois?" Amanda put on her best smile.

"Of course," Frank said, disappointed. He backed out of the room, lost his footing, and almost tripped. He straightened and then looked at the floor for the board sticking out that tripped him. "I'll . . . I'll be in the kitchen if you need me."

As Frank disappeared down the hall, Amanda looked Jason over and bestowed the same winning smile on him. Jason held her gaze. If eyes were windows to the soul, Jason liked what he saw.

"Why don't we sit down?" This was not the teenage reaction Amanda expected. She took a seat on a worn, dark-green easy chair. She pulled a large purse off her shoulder and placed it at her feet. Jason followed and settled with a grimace onto the couch opposite her.

"You're in pain," she said.

"Yeah." Jason leaned forward, finding it more comfortable. "Football," he said, holding his right side. "We played the Augies today."

"I see." Amanda looked around the room, dismissive of stupid sports injuries. Months of dust dulled the surfaces and objects littered about the room. She disapproved.

"So, Miss Rice," Jason said, wanting to get to the point.

"Yes," Amanda replied. She focused on Jason. "We have a mutual acquaintance. She is one of my clients. You know Sally Tilghman?"

Jason stared at her, surprised. Sally wasn't supposed to have any memory of him. Jason flashed back to the summer. Without any clear understanding of how, he had reversed Sally's suffering with Alzheimer's. In late August, he had detonated a memory bomb. It affected all people within a twenty-mile radius. Sally was supposed to be in the memory-alteration zone.

"She insisted," said Amanda. She placed her hands on her knees. "She wants to see you, now that she is back in Kearny."

"Where was she?" Jason asked, frantic that his identity could be compromised with this unfortunate twist of fate.

"At her daughter's in Harrisburg," Amanda said slowly. She frowned. "Is that important?"

"I'm sorry. I didn't expect to hear from her again."

"You and I both, Mr. Sutter, but . . ." She shrugged. "Here she is, clear-minded and asking for you."

"Yes," said Jason. Of course she would want to see him. "What do you suggest?"

Amanda reached down into her purse and pulled out her appointment book. "Sundays work best for me." She flipped pages back and forth. "How about two weeks from tomorrow?" She slid the pen from the binding. "Noon. I will pick you up at eleven." She looked up.

"Sundays are pretty much open for me too. I will have to check with Frank."

"Let's check now, shall we?" Amanda stood and moved to the hallway. Jason followed, slowly gasping for breath as pain shot front to back.

Frank dropped the newspaper he was reading and stood as Amanda entered the spotless kitchen. Jason came up behind her and explained the plan.

"Yeah, sure," Frank said, unable to object beneath her gaze.

"Great." Amanda thanked Frank and turned to go.

"Let me show you out," he insisted, moving to her side. Jason waved his good-bye and eased his aching body into a kitchen chair.

He heard the front door close and Frank's footsteps.

"Wow," he said, taking his seat. He picked up his paper. "So this Sally person was the one from the tabloid?"

"Yes, Frank," said Jason. "She's the one."

＊　　＊　　＊

Chet Winston leaned forward. He concentrated on the black-and-white, polished stone chessboard. His mind whirled. It worked feverishly to comprehend the possible outcomes, given the positions of the delicately shaped brass and pewter pieces on the field of battle.

Mark Woldham relaxed in the well-cushioned, expensively upholstered chair. The wooden arms and legs were intricately carved and lined in gold leaf. The chair reflected the room, a library awash in antique furniture and custom-made draperies. First-edition books from nineteenth-century authors lined the shelves. The ninety-year-old Woldham had spent years developing his wealth and his taste. He sat with his legs crossed and his elbows on the armrest; his fingertips touched. They hid his face except for his eyes, which were alight with victory at hand.

He sat up and leaned to one side to lift a glass of iced tea from a side table. He sipped, grateful for the hefty shot of rum. Watching the gears turn in the younger man's head, Woldham recognized a fellow predator. He had liked Chet from the day they met two weeks before. Who Chet targeted in his line of work he could not begin to guess. Woldham's victims were business competitors in a vicious market where the winner took all. He had amassed a fortune and sacrificed much to attain it. He had tried to fix matters by giving his children their inheritances. It did little to offset the years of neglect, but at least he got Christmas cards and an occasional letter. He still held a small fortune to maintain him until he died, albeit alone, except for Chet and others from the elder care group.

"I see no way out." Chet sat back. "You win again." Chet reached for his glass of iced tea, no extras, and lifted it in a salute to his opponent.

"It took much longer this time," Woldham said as he lifted his glass. "Good game." He took a long drink.

Chet liked this old guy; he was an interesting person. He did not whine. His other three near-used-up, well-to-do male clients complained about everything. Teenage-style angst over the unfairness of the world from adults of any age was abhorrent. Chet considered using his syringes on these men.

He smiled at Woldham, who made his job easier. He was still clear of mind and able to get around by himself. Chet also enjoyed their games of chess. At times, alone at night in his hotel room, Chet wondered why he did not feel like ridding the world of these aged men. Why did he target women exclusively? With clear insight, he grasped that his mother played a large part in his choice of targets. At this point, however, it didn't matter. It was what it was.

"Another game?" Chet reached for the pieces and placed them on the board.

"Why not," said Woldham. "Let's have some more tea, shall we?"

"Of course." Chet grinned. *Another loaded glass, and this bugger will be asleep for the rest of my shift.* Chet poured from the pitcher on the side table. He watched as Woldham emptied the last swallow of rum from a fifth bottle. This use of alcohol was reportable and probably caused problems with other medications the old guy took, but Chet looked the other way. Woldham had a right to enjoy the last of his life as he wished. *Besides,* thought Chet as he finished setting the field of play, *it made my life easier.*

"I wanted to ask you"—Chet paused as he took his seat—"do you know a Mrs. Tilghman?" He considered the reset board, thinking of an unconventional opening.

"Sally?" Woldham smiled as a happy memory replayed in his mind's eye. "Of course. We were good friends, almost engaged. Tilghman, however, put up the better fight for her hand." He leaned over when Chet took his opening position and moved the queen's pawn two spaces forward. "Why do you ask?"

"She has recovered." Chet placed his knight beyond the wall of pawns threatening Woldham's.

"Amazing. I've never heard of such a thing where Alzheimer's is concerned." His king's pawn moved up in support. "Is she out of the hospital and back in her home?"

"Her home?" asked Chet innocently. His king's pawn moved up two spaces.

"She lived on Prescott Street. Twenty-Three Prescott, if memory serves." He launched his queen-side knight onto the field. "That house is much too much for just one person. She'll need help like I do with this place."

"Twenty-Three Prescott Street," Chet repeated. He grinned; this was too easy. It was meant to be. He would not have to rifle the files at SeniorHomeAid. Soon Sally Tilghman would be dead, as she should be. With the rules reestablished and justice done, Chet could stand down for a while.

"Of course," said Woldham, taking a long swallow of his refreshed tea, "it has been a while. Is it the same Sally I knew?"

"Yes, Mr. Woldham," said Chet. "She's the one."

Chapter 7

In his hotel room, sitting in the comfortable, cushioned chair, Bill Sorenson casually scanned for psychic energy. He grunted when it happened and then went down on all fours and threw up. The blinding flash and the pain it delivered felt like he might be torn apart. The release of energy collapsed his abilities. It was like observing an atomic blast up close with no eye protection. Physically blind and psychically paralyzed, he fell over unconscious.

A mile away as Bill fell, Suzy felt the pull. She grabbed the kitchen counter and looked up through the window at the toolshed.

"Jason?" Suddenly, any action was impossible. She fell into one of the chairs around the kitchen table. She went unconscious just as her head hit her crossed arms. It was one o'clock in the afternoon, two hours after Amanda picked up Jason.

As Amanda pulled away from the curb in Franklin Chase, Chet Winston stood on the stoop of Sally Tilghman's house and knocked. *The day is perfect*, he thought. He turned to face the street, took a deep breath, and let it out slowly. Dried up, brown leaves bounced and flipped in the breeze over the lawns or skittered and clicked over the sidewalks and streets. The trees clung to their few remaining leaves, defiant in their descent into darkness. Chet smiled. *A perfect end to a perfect day.*

The worst whiner of his male clients, Ralph Diller, had pushed him one step too far. About an hour before, Chet had silenced the whining. It would be a few days before anyone found the body hanging by the neck in the basement. Chet laughed through the whole brutal action, warning the man to shut up. He did not, of course, complaining loudly about Chet's poor performance and promising a putative call to management.

Chet grabbed him by the back of his pajama's collar and dragged him downstairs. The victim's ineffectual, weak arms and legs flailed. The wrinkled, veined hands grasped the rope dropped around his neck and tried to pull it away from his neck as Chet hoisted him up from a rafter. The old guy struggled, but his remaining strength failed. Chet got comfortable on the steps and watched. When Diller's leg trembling subsided, he realized that time was wasting away. His devotion to universal justice demanded that he get moving to his next, more important task.

He turned and smiled pleasantly when he heard the door open behind him.

"Yes?" Sally held the door open a hand's width. She looked her visitor over and took comfort that this stranger wore the SeniorHomeAid blue jumpsuit. The door opened further.

"Mrs. Tilghman?" Chet pulled a memo pad from the top pocket of his suit. He flipped pages. When the old lady said nothing, he stopped on a blank page, looked up, and smiled. "Nurse Rice asked me to check in on you before I ended my shift today."

"Oh? She won't keep our planned meeting at twelve?" When Sally's disappointment registered on her face, Chet almost laughed.

"No, no." Thinking quickly, he added, "She will be here, just a bit late." He had no idea about Amanda's plans for the day. He hoped violence would not be needed so early in his and Sally's relationship.

"With Mr. Sutter?" Sally smiled.

"Yes, of course." Chet wondered who this guy might be. He realized that he may never know, given his plans for the next hour. He moved closer to the door. "Nurse Rice thought I could keep you company until they arrive."

"You are?" asked Sally. This man aroused her suspicions. Amanda would have done the common-sense thing; she would have called.

"Chet Winston, ma'am. Just following orders, ma'am."

Chet's ear-to-ear grin sent a chill through her whole body; her internal alarms sounded.

Chet charged when she started to shut the door. His impact kicked the heavy door inward. It hit Sally's forehead, leaving her stunned. Chet forced his way in as Sally fell back, collapsing on the floor. He shot into the house, slamming the door shut behind him. A roll of duct tape came out. Chet lifted her easily like a groom carrying his beloved across the threshold. They went upstairs to her bedroom. Each step taken in the silent house was to a Beethoven crescendo in Chet's mind. Tears flowed down his cheeks. The moment could not be more perfect, more godlike.

✫   ✫   ✫

Jason waited patiently at the curb. Amanda's white Ford Galaxy arrived precisely on time for the ride to Kearny. Frank waved good-bye on the front porch of the huge, old Victorian house. Jason sensed his disappointment that Amanda would not join him for coffee before hitting the road.

Poor Frank. Jason shook his head. Frank could not compete with this woman's drive to get the job done, any job. Once the car pulled away from the curb and the usual polite conversation had been used up, conversation ended.

Amanda wondered what Sally saw in this kid, who was nothing special as far as she could tell. He couldn't keep up his end of an adult conversation.

Jason, on the other hand, considered strategies for dealing with Sally Tilghman's intact memories of his abilities and how they had saved her. He worked every option, allowing her stay as she was. None left Jason secure and Sally safe if Jason's enemies sensed her knowledge of him. He sadly came to the obvious conclusion. Her memory needed modification, but he would be as gentle as possible.

With his plan decided, he watched the landscape fly by. He had had a fantastic week. His path to his ultimate goal had opened before him. The good times had started on the previous Saturday, when his team beat the Renquist Academy team. The Hoover Jaguars were not supposed to beat the private school's superior team and financial advantages. Artie's and his play proved to be too much for them. But on Sunday he got caught completely by surprise.

Jason dragged himself down to the kitchen. He hurt all over from Saturday's game and needed aspirin or something to ease his suffering. He walked into a kitchen filled with the house residents. They sat around the kitchen table, grinning at him. In one voice they yelled and sang, "Happy birthday to you . . ."

There was a cake and all the trimmings. He struggled to keep control, amazed by their tenderness toward him.

To top it off, on Wednesday evening Brother Michaels showed up at the house and pulled him away from a boring homework assignment. With Frank in the conversation, he started talking about Jason attending St. Augustine High School with a full scholarship. Jason had hardly paid attention after the first ten minutes. He knew it was a ploy to get him to play football for their school.

When the discussion turned to college, however, it became interesting. Brother Michaels discussed how 98 percent of St. Augustine students went to college. He described their superior course offerings and their help with the Scholastic Achievement Tests, or SATs. Suddenly all ears, Jason discovered that this was the test to get into college. A single test would open the door to college.

Take this test and get into a New York College flashed across Jason's thoughts. *Do incredible on this test and get to your mother in New York.* His sudden excitement convinced both Frank and Brother Michaels that he wanted to attend St. Augustine. Jason let them believe what they wanted while he discovered where the test was offered and when. In December he would be able to take the SAT if Frank funded it. Jason worked that angle, realizing he might have to use his psychic abilities to move Frank in the right direction. He hoped it would not come to that. He would not hesitate, however, to do anything to get to his mother's side and help.

"Mr. Sutter." Amanda interrupted his reverie. "Mrs. Tilghman calls you her angel. Why would she think that?"

"I don't know," he said staring out the window. "I guess . . ."

"You guess what?" she said.

"Mrs. Tilghman somehow sees me as having helped her."

"I see." The conversation ended. The car accelerated.

It was not long before Amanda turned onto Prescott Street in Kearny. In the distance, a few blocks away, a gray car turned a corner and disappeared. Jason did not give it much thought.

Amanda killed the engine. "This is the place. C'mon."

They stood at the door and waited after pressing the button and hearing the doorbell sound inside the house. Amanda banged on the heavy wood when there was no answer.

"Maybe she's out back in the garden." She had turned to check the back of the house when Jason reached out to try the knob. The door swung open. They looked at each other, sensing trouble.

"Hello, Sally!" called Amanda from the threshold. There was no answer. She moved into the living room and then to the kitchen beyond. Jason hung back; he had a clear sense of Sally from the first time they met. Something bad had happened; it scared him.

"I'm going to the back door to check the garden," called Amanda from the kitchen. "You sit tight. I'll be right back."

Jason ignored her. He felt sure that something had happened upstairs. He climbed the steps; Amanda called for Sally from the backyard. At the door to the second room on the right, he stopped. The door was ajar. He peered in and saw the bed unmade.

"Mrs. Tilghman?" he whispered as he walked into the room, scanning the terrain. "Mrs. Tilghman?" he called louder. His heart hammered as he stepped past an armoire to reach and open a door. It was a large walk-in closet full of clothes. Jason squatted to look beneath the hanging dresses to be certain they hid nothing. A hand grasped his shoulder. Without thinking, he dove forward and turned on his haunches, ready to fight.

"I asked you to sit tight." Amanda looked over the closet. "If she is here, she might not be alone. It could be dangerous to search alone."

Jason calmed himself. "She's here somewhere. I know it." He stood up and walked back into the bedroom. "Next time make some noise, will ya?"

"How do you know?" Amanda followed, frustrated by the situation and worried that Sally might be hurt. She had no patience for the sensitivities of adolescents and their magical thinking.

"I just do." Jason stood before the armoire. This adult was getting on his nerves. He touched the door, and it opened as Sally Tilghman's body spilled out on to the floor. Jason lost all control. He screamed in anguish. Amanda knelt, turned her over, and checked her body for vital signs.

"Goddamn it!" yelled Amanda. Sally was dead. Amanda was sure she had fallen prey to the killer she knew was out there. She had failed to make the case and convince the right people. Her failure killed her patient, her friend. "Goddamn it!" She cradled the body in her arms, sobbing quietly.

Tears streamed down Jason's cheeks. "No," he commanded in a whisper.

Energy gathered and flowed in from every living person Jason could reach; it cascaded into him. He didn't care if he was found out. He took Sally's lifeless hand in his and started.

"I will remember you, young man," echoed Sally's voice from their first meeting. Jason brought all his abilities to bear. The mechanics kicked on first: the heart pumped and blood circulated. In her mind, Jason pushed through the doors into a dark room where once he had found lights. He, however, had been there before, knew what to do, and possessed a thousand times more power.

"Sally! Sally! Show me!" Jason waited.

Amanda did not believe in miracles. She had faith only in a bloodied hand that reached beyond the rib spreader to massage a still heart back to life. That was her reality. When Sally Tilghman's chest rose and fell, reality turned upside down. There was a pulse. The boy knelt opposite her. With eyes closed, he held Sally's hand, and Amanda thought she saw an aura where they touched. The effect lasted only minutes. Finally, the boy released her and then collapsed. Amanda looked down and realized that she no longer held a corpse. Sally looked peacefully asleep.

"You were dead." Amanda shook her head. "How?" Disbelieving her own eyes, she stared at the unconscious boy on the floor. The light pat on her arm startled her. Sally's bright blue eyes looked up at her. Leaning close, Amanda heard her whisper.

"Help my angel, Amanda."

Chapter 8

Amanda trembled. She clutched her black cup of coffee, focusing on this small piece of solid reality, an anchor. The rest of her world spun wildly into nonsense. Jason and Amanda sat opposite each other at the island in Sally's kitchen.

Jason rested his head on his crossed arms. He had never felt this used up. Sally slept peacefully in her bed.

"Can you tell me what happened?" Amanda closed her eyes. There had been no vitals. "She was dead." She opened them and waited for the boy's answer. He had been unconscious for over an hour on the bedroom floor before he stirred. After another thirty minutes, Amanda was able to pull him to his feet and help him downstairs to the kitchen. She watched him intently as he looked up at her and did the one thing she could not comprehend: he smiled.

"I am revealed," Jason said, sensing her confusion and fear. He could show her more. It did not matter anymore, since there was a huge afterglow, a huge sign over Kearny stating that he was there. "The game has started in earnest now."

"Just tell me what's going on!" She was losing control.

In response, the sugar bowl danced across the countertop untouched. Amanda stared at it, appalled. She fought her first impulse to run.

"I can do things." Jason tapped his right temple. "That is how Sally knows me. We had a meeting of the minds at the hospital." Jason's head fell back down. "I couldn't let her go, after what happened then. Just couldn't."

"What are you?" asked Amanda, recalling the tabloid cover.

"I don't know, but I am trying like crazy to find out."

With those words, Amanda the professional, the nurse, the healer took the common-sense approach. She calmed and considered what she had just observed and heard.

"What does 'I am revealed' mean?"

✵   ✵   ✵

Bill Sorenson regained consciousness after several hours and gathered his strength for the search-and-destroy mission. By four o'clock he was on the road to Kearny, following the clear signposts to his target.

Bill burst through the front door on Prescott Street, his defenses in full-on mode. He was untouchable by his kind. He came up short when he found Jason and Amanda sitting side by side on the living room couch, at their ease.

"At last," said Jason. He sat forward, his hands clasped in front of him. "We've been waiting for you." He paused, making the effort to hide his weakened condition. Although he felt much better, he knew he was no match for the person sent to track him down in a one-on-one confrontation. "I have been aware of you for quite some time. I would like this cat-and-mouse game to end."

Bill relaxed but remained vigilant. "You know why I am here?"

"Of course. Now that you have found me, what do you intend?" Jason watched his every move. He was not sure he could shield himself from a determined attack. He pulled energy from Amanda, who had agreed fearlessly to help after he told her everything about his hospital encounter with Sally. She recognized that they shared the same desire to make things better.

"Found you?" Bill stood just inside the door. He studied the details of the room, seeking the trap. "Who are you?"

"Use your gifts. Tell me who I am." Jason did not use his to reach out to touch the man. He would not start the battle, if there was to be one.

Bill felt uneasy. He knew he was missing something. "You, young man, and your lady friend are of no concern to me. You are normal."

"Really?" Jason could not believe his luck. *He can't see me.*

"Where is your master, your benefactor?" demanded Bill. Normal people had been used on occasion for Community business. They were especially good at taking care of children.

"Do you need more help from me?" asked Amanda.

"A little maybe," said Jason. He turned to Bill, who could not protect himself from what he could not sense. He forced Bill forward like a reluctant toddler pushed from behind by his parent. The man walked into the living room and took a seat on the ottoman next to the couch.

Too late, Bill comprehended his situation.

I think, Mr. Sorenson, it is time for you to return home and report.

Jason got home late, because Amanda took a short knap on Sally's living-room couch before climbing behind the wheel. He had used her up. On the road to Franklin Chase, they worked out a plan for dealing with Sally's assailant. Jason had spread out a mental net, looking for killing images, and had located his man at his motel. Justice would be meted out very soon. In front of the big Victorian house, they agreed on the place and time for their next meeting.

Amanda pulled away from the curb as Jason waved from the porch. She headed back to Kearny to follow up with Sally.

The front door closed as he walked into the house, and Suzy bounded into him and pinned his arms in a desperate hug. "I thought you were dead!" Tears flowed. "I can't stand not knowing. You gotta let me know you're okay."

Frank walked from the kitchen with the Sunday paper in his hands. He looked quizzically at Jason and then at Suzy with her arms wrapped around him. She was obviously crying. Jason gently extracted himself from Suzy's hug. She kept a firm grip on his hand.

"She was worried," he said. "It was getting late." He shrugged.

Frank nodded, knowing that there was no accounting for teenage angst. "How did it go in Kearny?" he asked as he started up the first steps and stopped.

"It went well, Frank." Jason smiled. "I met with Mrs. Tilghman. She's doing fine."

Frank stopped. "Well?"

"Amanda asked about you," Jason lied.

"Oh, did she?" Frank smiled slightly, trying to show that it made no difference. The spring in his step as he headed toward his room said otherwise. From the top step, as he pulled a newspaper section from the middle and put it on top for immediate consideration, he said, "We saved some dinner for you. It's in the oven. I am sure Suzy, if she lets you go, can help."

Suzy threw her arms around Jason again when Frank disappeared upstairs. Surprised and annoyed with her reaction, Jason untwined himself, although part of him fought letting her go. He took her hand and led her to the kitchen.

Once there, he said, "I need you to do me a favor."

"Promise, first." Suzy confronted Jason, pulling back. They faced each other.

"Promise what?"

"If you are going to do anything dangerous, let me know. I collapsed when you pulled the strength out of me. What happened? I can't stand it." More tears were imminent.

"Okay, I promise. I did not plan anything. Stuff just happened." Jason took her other hand. "I need you to call Russ and see if we can get him over here for an hour or so right now. Will you do that for me?" For a person with great power, Jason felt sheepish and uncomfortable touching and being touched by Suzy. He let her hands go and watched her go to the front room to make the call. He shook his head. "Girls."

Russ struck the match and lit the candles in the toolshed. The days were getting shorter as Halloween approached. He pulled the door closed and wedged it shut with a stick. The meeting was top secret, so they needed as much privacy as possible.

"So," said Russ as he dragged up his stool and sat, "what have you got?"

Jason raised his hand and ticked off the list on his fingers. "I saved Sally Tilghman . . . again; interrogated the black car driver and sent him home; let another adult know about me; and I am tracking a serial killer of the elderly." He paused. "Oh, yeah, and I have sort of a plan for getting to my mom, but it needs more work." As an afterthought, he added, "The Jaguars are having their first winning season."

"Time for the details," said Suzy. "Start at the beginning."

Jason described his whole Sunday. He left nothing out. When he finished, they sat staring at the candle flames.

"Okay, the guy watching my house is gone," Russ said. "Good. What did you send him home to do?" Russ looked past Suzy at Jason.

"The old guy who attacked Patti takes the blame. Bill Sorenson, the guy watching your house, will confirm that it was a big mistake. The boss or bosses or whoever will go after the old guy for answers." Jason rubbed his eyes, still worn out from the day's efforts.

Russ thought a minute. "Okay, what'd you learn from him?"

"Only a few things, but they are important." Jason rested his elbows on the workbench; he entwined his fingers as if in prayer. "I got into Sorenson's mind, but there were places I could not open." He turned to Suzy. "It was the same kind of block I get from you. I didn't have enough power to break through." He recalled that Amanda had keeled over on the couch about that time. "What I managed to discover is that there are whole groups of people like me. They're called Communities. They had this big war about fifteen years ago. Many in the Communities were killed." Jason looked from Suzy to Russ. "Chiang and Downing were right. The wrong side won." His eyes settled on Russ. "Something you should know."

Shocked, Russ instinctively looked over his shoulder as though Jason meant the imaginary guy standing behind him.

Jason continued. "I saw the picture of what he saw hovering over your house. Patti is pretty much invisible. You, however, show up a brighter color than your mom. Your whole family is like us, only on the weaker side except for Patti . . . maybe you."

Russ stared blankly, than a big grin expanded on his face.

"I think," Jason said, "you are like Suzy in what you can do. Maybe that is why I didn't sense your abilities sooner. It means I had twice the number of batteries I needed to get the job done back in August."

"I'm one of you," Russ whispered. The sudden rush of emotion caught him by surprise. He coughed, not sure whether he might laugh or cry.

Suzy put her hand on his arm and squeezed. "You'll get used to it."

Their meeting came to an end a short time later. Russ's eyes glazed over; he stopped listening. Jason had not expected that reaction. Both Jason and Suzy were worried about their friend, so they walked him home.

"There is no point in hiding anymore," Jason said as they took shortcuts through backyards and between houses. "I need better help to figure out what to do."

Suzy stated the obvious. "You will take this special test, do extremely well, and somehow get to New York to save her." Hearing it was different, however, than thinking it. It became real.

"Yes. That's the plan." They climbed over a short fence and walked up the alley that led to their street. "How to get to New York will require a great deal of thought."

On the porch, Suzy asked, "How long will you be gone, or am I going with you?"

Jason came up short. He had not considered Suzy in his plan. "I guess . . . I will be gone long enough to get my mom to safety and then healthy enough to take care of herself. I don't know how long that will take." He remembered the hug earlier. "Maybe a month or two?"

Suzy nodded. She grabbed his hand and gave it a never-let-me-go squeeze. Jason felt it, absorbed it, and held her hand equally tight. They entered the house together.

"No longer," she commanded. They disconnected and calmly went upstairs.

✻   ✻   ✻

Reena Sorenson grabbed the hall phone on the wall just outside the kitchen. She held the glossy, green handset as if she were about to bang it against the wall. Two calls to the room and hotel desk had produced nothing. She hung up. There was no one to call. Her link to Bill was gone. Frantic, Reena would not be consoled by the fact that it had been only a few minutes.

The link suddenly reappeared. The phone rang.

"What happened?" She contained her relief, falling into her all-business mode.

"I'm not sure." Bill sounded weary. "It's happened before when I overdrive myself. Maybe that's what happened. One minute I am scanning the local terrain. The next it all goes dark, and I am as helpless as a normal."

"You pushed too hard . . . for me." Reena knew he would give his all. She did not expect it to cost him so much. "You need to sleep for a while. What have you learned?"

"I will, hon." Bill laid back on the bed in his hotel room. Her voice was so soothing. "Rodney screwed up big time. The girl's a normal. There's nothing special about the family except for the mother. She's pretty weak and not worth our notice. What made him attack is beyond me."

"Rodney is out of the way. Samantha has taken over." Reena leaned back against the wall and smiled. "Time to come home, my dear."

"I will sleep, then dash back to you. I will see you tomorrow night. Keep the lights on for me." He sat up. "Love you. See you soon."

"Love you too."

Bill hung up and immediately collapsed back on the bed and slept. He dreamed of going home. When the front door of his Bismarck house swung open, it was a smiling Elizabeth Sutter who greeted him. Bill snapped awake in a sweat. It was dark outside his window.

"Where did that come from?" he whispered, holding his head. His heart pounded. He got up and splashed cold water on his face in the bathroom. He felt unsettled. On the way back to the bed, a vague memory of feeling sick and lying on the floor flashed into his mind. He stopped and considered it. The last time this had happened was during the war. Was this a flashback? It happened from time to time.

The clock read four in the morning. He would not get back to sleep. After packing and settling the bill at the front desk, he headed to the Philadelphia airport. *The sooner I'm home, the better*, he thought. He set aside the dream and the flashback.

Reena would help him sort it out.

Chapter 9

Bill arrived home on Monday, late in the evening. He and Reena clung to each other desperately for hours after his return to the nest. A few days later, Bill slaved gleefully in his woodworking shop. The saw spun, the router tore elegant shapes magically in raw wood rectangles, and he constructed the finished piece to the blueprints in his head: a mahogany, highboy dresser. He was home, the harmony of his life restored. Awareness of his wife, no longer far away, snuggled comfortably in his mind. He whistled and hummed, unaware he did so as his hands caressed and slid over the smooth, styled pieces.

Reena cried. She sat at her kitchen table unable to hold back her sorrow. She and Bill had sorted out his concerns; he had allowed her to dig into his thoughts and memories. There were changes, subtle modifications. Their camouflage was almost perfect against Bill's mental terrain. Reena had almost missed them; they aligned with her desired expectations. When she set aside what she hoped to find, she discovered the faint shadows of a different reality. Which was real?

Reena wiped away the tears and straightened up. Clearing her mind of personal issues, she took a deep breath. With her superior abilities and rational leadership as the ruler of all Communities, she assessed the situation without emotion. Bill had been compromised by a great, singular force. Someone did what she could not. Reena could only read the signs left behind. The mental version of a bent branch or footprint in the mud pointed to a person of unquestioned ability. She could not focus the partial, fuzzy images of two people seated on a living-room sofa or a front-page newspaper picture. There was, however, one image in both: a boy.

Reena did not tell Bill about what she found. She would in time. Now a plan to deal with the boy consumed her.

✫   ✫   ✫

Amanda Rice and Jason sat across from each other over her desk at the SeniorHomeAid office. She had picked him up as planned, and now they went over the final details of their plan for justice.

"There will not be much for you to do," said Jason. He sat back with one leg crossed over the other. "It will be like watching a movie or TV show."

"You can take what you want and do what you will with his or anyone's mind?" Amanda's medically trained mind still fought her observations: Sally lived and the sugar bowl moved untouched. *But how can this be?*

"Yes." Jason watched Amanda look away through the windows to the parking lot. Her hands moved constantly; she pulled back her hair, pulled open a drawer, and searched her pockets for no reason. "If this is too hard for you, then—"

"No. I want to know." She calmed herself and stopped moving. "I want to understand what you are."

"All I can say is bring an open, analytic perspective and relax. You will see what I see in your mind's eye." Jason smiled. "It may be entertaining." He stood and frowned. "Remember, you were right. He murdered people you cared for. It does not matter that he stole only a minute, an hour, or a week of life."

Amanda nodded, rose, and picked up her purse. "I'm ready. Let's settle this."

They left the office side by side.

✫   ✫   ✫

Chet had no intention of leaving Kearny until he basked in the news reports of two murders with the baffled police tearing apart the crime scene to find no clues. They would, of course, come looking for Chet Winston as the possible last person to see the victims alive. Mr. Diller's appointment was logged in the SeniorHomeAid books, and Chet's name was next to it.

But Chet, like his former alias, Mortimer, no longer existed. Jack Smith had replaced Chet. Jack changed to a new motel, which he planned to be his launch site out of Pennsylvania to someplace else, some other state.

He studied a map of Maryland, holding it out like a newspaper while listening to the local news report on the radio next to the bed. As he considered his next destination, he lay propped up with pillows in bed, wearing a white T-shirt and jeans, his bare feet crossed. He studied the map by lamplight; the heavy curtains blocked the late morning sunlight.

> *The police chief announced today that a Mr. Ralph Diller, an elderly, long-time resident of Kearny, was found dead in his basement. The police suspect foul play and are searching for a missing SeniorHomeAid staff person for questioning. In the meantime, they are combing the suspected crime scene for clues. When asked why the police think Mr. Diller was murdered, the chief stated, "Mr. Diller, according to records, was too weak to hang himself." The police chief said he would provide an update as soon as possible. In other news . . .*

"One down." Jack folded the map and smiled at the green glow of the dial. He was a little concerned that Sally Tilghman's death had not yet been announced. Nurse Rice should have found her last Sunday, and here it was Saturday. Assuming she found Sally, why didn't she call the police?

The knock on the door surprised him.

"Edward Steadman," yelled a woman's voice, "you useless piece of crap, you open this door this instant!"

Jack Smith evaporated. Edward Steadman lay shaking in his motel bed with a Maryland map crunched in his shaking hands. He froze, paralyzed by fear of two things: no one in Pennsylvania knew his real name and the sound of his dead mother's voice. Killed when the house in which he grew up burned down, the Steadman family members had been Eddie's first victims.

"Open this door, young man, or I'll whip your sorry little butt so you won't sit for a year." The door shook with a heavy pound.

Eddie's anger erupted and took over when he thought of his loser family, especially his witch of a mother. No longer a child but a man—a strong man who could take a life with ease—he jumped from the bed to the door. Whoever was banging would get the full force of his violence.

He jerked the door open to catch whoever it was by surprise. No one was there. Leaning over the threshold, Edward looked left and right down the row of doors. His car in front and a white Ford close to the office were the only ones on that side of the motel. He stared at the white car, trying to recall if he knew anyone who drove one. No one came to mind.

Stepping outside, he ran his hand through his hair and looked across the way to the rusted, chain-link fence marking the property line between the motel and the empty, overgrown lot beyond. Nothing.

Eddie rubbed his eyes and turned back to his room. Confused, he shut the door behind him and shot the deadbolt home. When the toilet flushed and his dead mother walked out of the bathroom, he slammed back into the door, eyes wide. She wore the same stained, bright-yellow, flowered muumuu: a tablecloth with holes for a head and arms that barely covered her folds of skin. Fear electrocuted Eddie's body like lightning strikes; his extremities sizzled with the terror.

"Never thought you'd see me again. Isn't that right, Eddie?" She walked up to the mirror over the worn dresser, smoothed out her yellow dress, and brushed her long, silver hair. "Nothing to say there, Chief?"

Eddie moaned. No one called him Chief except his demented mother. She had humiliated him constantly with that nickname, reminding him and anyone nearby that on a Halloween when he was ten years old, he returned home having been bullied out of his bag of candy. Eddie had worn an Indian costume with feathers sticking out of his hair and war paint on his face.

"What a little, worthless coward!" she had yelled at him. "Get back out there and get back what's yours."

He was beaten up by the bigger boys and returned with no candy, a bloodied nose, and a big wet spot on the front of his fringed, imitation cowhide pants. Afterward, whenever she wanted to hurt him, she called him Chief Piss-in-Pants, which in time shortened to Chief.

Eddie turned around and grabbed the doorknob desperate to escape this nightmare; the door refused to budge. Every all-out pull was resisted; every begging tear born of fear was ignored.

"Give it a rest, Eddie." She bounced back on the bed. The springs groaned. "Ya know, I woke up coughing from the smoke. My beautiful dress caught fire." Thoughtful for a second, she continued. "Hurt something awful for a time." She paused. "Of course, it's not just me who has an ax to grind with you."

Eddie leaned his head against the unyielding door. His head rapped the brown metal surface, trying to expunge this rabid hallucination.

"You!" screamed a familiar voice. "You sonovabitch! You, you . . ." A man's angry voice filled the room. Eddie Steadman had to look. He turned slowly and saw Mr. Diller standing by his mother, pointing at a swollen-knuckled index finger. He was still in his silk, dark-blue pajamas, and his fury produced a fiery glow around his head.

"Mr. Diller," said Eddie's mother, "if I might impose on your good graces, I need to have a few words with my worthless son."

The old man glanced down at his fellow traveler. He dropped his arm. "Of course, my dear."

"We're all here, Chief. All of us." She stood by Mr. Diller as Eddie's other victims paraded from the bathroom.

Eddie howled like a cruelly wounded animal. He turned and clawed at the door for escape. The door finally cooperated: the lock opened by itself; the knob turned. The crazed man flew into the sunlit parking lot. Barefoot, he ran past the white Ford to the front of the motel, then into the street. Cars honked and brakes screeched to avoid hitting the nutcase who had come out of nowhere. He made it to the other side and kept on going. Arms flailing, screaming at the top of his lungs, Eddie raced away.

Jason watched from the motel lobby through the floor-to-ceiling, plate-glass window. Amanda sat with eyes closed in one of the lobby chairs until Jason released her. She rose and stood by his side at the window.

When the man Amanda knew as Chet Winston made it across the busy street, she turned to Jason.

"What now?"

"Time to call the police." Jason followed her to the reception desk. She made the anonymous call. Between the evidence kept in an attaché case in the room and Eddie's new, constant companions, his killing spree was over.

"He really killed all those people?" asked Amanda as she hung up the phone. The children in the crowd confronting their murderer upset her.

"Yes." Jason held her gaze and made a more direct psychic connection. She deserved a reward for her constant fight for the good of her charges— wounded soldiers or the elderly.

"You could have killed him easily and saved everyone a lot of trouble," Amanda said.

"Edward Steadman is a very dangerous but very sick man." Jason showed her what he thought. She gasped at the intimacy of his thoughts sliding in and around hers. This was different from watching from the sidelines as ghosts came and went in Eddie's mind.

I don't want to kill anybody. Jason sensed that Amanda felt his feelings and understood the mental illness driving Edward Steadman. When she nodded, Jason eased his mind out of hers.

"Time to get back to Sally." Jason needed to see Sally alive and well.

Amanda smiled but could not look at him. She felt totally exposed, like being naked in front of strangers. It took time to shake it off. "Absolutely," she said pushing aside her embarrassment. She faced Jason. "Justice has been served."

✳   ✳   ✳

Dr. Lipton sat at his office desk. His jacket hung on the back of the chair. The top button of his shirt was open and his red and blue striped tie was pulled down. His fingers flipped through the weeks of mail piled up on his desk. Pipe smoke filled the office, and he endeavored with the pipe tight between his teeth to thicken the haze.

Lipton had just returned from a two-week vacation. Most of the letters and advertisements flew into the brown wastepaper can by his desk. As he was about to send another advertisement to the bin, he stopped and opened it. The tastefully drawn page was an invitation for papers to be given at a local American Psychiatric Association (APA) chapter meeting. The place for the meeting more than the subject matter caught his eye: Poughkeepsie, New York. Jason Sutter's sad face at their final appointment came to mind, plus the letter stating that an Elizabeth Sutter was an in-patient at Poughkeepsie State Hospital.

He pulled his pipe from his lips, leaned back in his chair, and crossed his arms. He argued with himself about which action made better sense. His pipe pointed in one direction and then in the other as the discussion progressed. Finally, the doctor sat forward, set his pipe in its holder, and reached for a piece of paper. He pulled his fountain pen from his desk drawer and wrote two letters. One went to the psychiatric department head, his boss, announcing that he would attend the APA meeting in May. He was allowed two such professional get-togethers per year. The second went to Jason Sutter. Lipton hoped to replace his memory of a sad Jason with a happier one.

✳   ✳   ✳

On the same day that Lipton caught up with his mail, Mrs. Lim slid an unopened envelope in front of Chiang Chen as he sat at the kitchen table, sipping tea. He put his cup in the saucer and looked up at her questioningly.

"From the embassy in Washington, D.C." She patted his shoulder. "If you need my help . . ." She smiled and left the room. He knew where to find her.

Chiang opened the envelope and discovered he had an appointment at the Chinese embassy in Washington in two weeks. There was no explanation. He knew he had no choice if he wanted to stay in the United States and finish the full term of the agreement between Pennsylvania State University and his government. He stood and went to the back porch overlooking the barren, winter-ready garden. Mrs. Lim sat on the porch, wrapped in a thick woolen sweater; her hands worked deftly to break some vegetable into smaller pieces for cooking.

"This is not something to be concerned about," she said. She did not appear upset in the least, but focused on her hands as they performed their steady task. "It has happened with all of you who have been in this country for any length of time."

"It is only routine then?" Chiang walked over to where she worked, and leaned against the porch railing opposite her.

"Yes and no." Mrs. Lim finished with the last piece and then slapped her hands together to remove any vegetable remnants. She put the bowl on the floor by her feet. She looked up at Chiang. "They will ask if your efforts have produced anything useful for our country." She raised her hand to silence Chiang before he listed his accomplishments. "It is not their true goal. What they truly want to know is if you intend to stay in the United States."

"They fear I would abandon my country?" Chiang acted shocked but knew the political paranoia of his government's leaders.

"It has happened before, too many times." She stood, picked up the bowl, and started for the kitchen. "Show them what you have shown me. I do not doubt your intentions." She disappeared into the house. Chiang followed, holding the letter in one hand and running his fingers through his hair with the other.

"How long will it take to prove my worthiness?"

"You should plan on being in Washington for three to four weeks." Mrs. Lim ran water over the bowl's contents.

"So long?"

Mrs. Lim looked at him, saying nothing. Chiang was not so naïve or so politically unaware that he could not see how the time might be stretched out. He nodded, acquiescing to the unavoidable. This was not personal. He would be able to attend one more meeting at the library with Downing, Louise, and Mary to push Jason's career forward another inch, and Downing and Mary's wedding the following week.

Chiang had not seen Jason in weeks. The boy claimed to keep up with his meditations, but Chiang knew other attractions distracted him:

football not the least. He wondered if Jason was doing well and having a good time. Was he pushing his limits to reach a higher state of mind?

Letting the kitchen door close behind him, Chiang went back on the porch and sat in the chair vacated by Mrs. Lim. He still grasped the letter, fretted, and looked out at the backyard. Far back, near the wooden fence, dead, brown stems waved in a light breeze. Chiang's brow wrinkled. Those flowers should not have grown in this place.

"I know how I got here." He stood and addressed the brown stems. "How did you?"

Chapter 10

On the first Saturday in December, Jason walked into the huge, yellow-brick gymnasium on the local, state college campus. There were two hundred student desks arrayed in ten rows of twenty. A few test takers sat in the seats, waiting the remaining minutes before the testing began. He chose to sit near the front of the pack. Newspapers covered the moderator's desk beneath the basketball backboard. Some of the waiting students had their own and were reading intently.

The news had come fast and furious of the assassination of President Kennedy and then of the unexpected killing of the assassin, Lee Harvey Oswald, by Jack Ruby. Jason recalled the early dismissal from school and sitting around the kitchen table with the older kids, listening to the radio announcer confirm that John F. Kennedy was dead. In shock, the country mourned.

Jason felt bad for his friend Downing. He and Mary Del Oro married the weekend after the president's fateful trip to Dallas. The two were inextricably connected. The very tasteful ceremony took place at Mary and Louise's home. It was a mansion surrounded by well-tended, sprawling gardens, now bear with the coming winter. The ceremony in the solarium rose and fell with emotion like a symphony. The cooperative sun provided a beautiful afternoon glow. The knot was tied before thirty clapping witnesses when the preacher at the wedding's crescendo turned the two to face the audience and introduced them for the first time as Mr. and Mrs. Downing.

Russ did his best to dance with Suzy and other girls who attended, but stepped on more than a few toes. He confided to Jason that he intended to practice before he went to another wedding. Jason did better dancing with Mary, while Downing danced with Suzy. Chiang moved across the floor with Louise as though they danced on air. Besides indulging in several large pieces of wedding cake, Jason had his first taste of wine. He waved at Miss Thompson who sat at the head table. She was Downing's God daughter and the person who introduced Jason to the library. She raised her glass acknowledging Jason.

An older man with wispy, white hair but startling blue eyes tapped his wine glass to get everyone's attention and introduced himself as Colonel Ramsey Steele, retired. "Mary, our Major Downing is an interesting man," he said. "You will need eyes to the front and rear to keep track of his interests." Steele smiled broadly, noting that Downing gave him his full attention. "England during the war provided a very ripe field for the major's . . . feminine conquests." He waited for the chuckling to die down. "He is also a man I am proud to call my friend. I am intensely happy that he has found you, and I salute your choice and good judgment." He raised his glass. "Congratulations to you both. May you never have a snafu." In a commanding voice, he proclaimed, "No 'Situation Normal All.'" Colonel Steele winked at Downing. "To the happy couple!"

After the first taste, Jason sipped the remainder of the champagne as waves of toasts and glasses clinking for Downing to kiss Mary took over the room. He did not like wine. It tasted like vinegar and was very salty. He scanned the room and watched as empty glasses were immediately refilled by a diligent staff. Obviously, normal people did not share his experience.

Jason set his glass down and looked around for Suzy to dance. Chiang sat next to him. "A lovely ceremony," he said. "I think they are well suited after all the time they have spent together at the library."

"I hope so." Jason recalled the Kyle Downing who demolished him playing game after game of ping-pong, even after he was covered with splattered paint, diving for the ball. Mary, however, could apply spin with the best of them. She would keep the old man on his toes. Jason smiled, remembering Mary with Downing in the library. Then he said, "Yes, you're right."

"I also came over to let you know I will be going away for a month, maybe less. I must attend to an issue at our embassy in Washington."

Jason nodded. "You'll be coming back, right?"

"That is my plan."

"Gentlemen, less talk more dance." Rebecca Thompson walked up to them. Her ivory gown flowed with each step giving the impression that her feet never touched the ground. Suzy followed in her wake. "Professor Chen, you owe me a spin on the floor." Suzy took Jason's hand and pulled him up. "I expect to be asked for a dance." She looked at Jason who nodded.

"I will look for you when I return," called Chiang as he moved away to the strains of a waltz.

"Suzy, you look really good . . . pretty. I mean pretty." Jason placed his hand on her back and clasped her hand. She smiled at his awkwardness. It was endearing, given that he might be the most powerful being on earth.

Awaiting the start of the SAT, Jason realized that November would forever bring back these happy, wonderful moments but also the death of a beloved president.

Every desk possessed a resident as the test start time drew near. Jason lined up the extra No. 2 pencils and a large, pink eraser on the right side of the desk. He did not expect to use the eraser; his coaches, Downing, Mary, Louise, and Chiang insisted. Frank did what he could to help, but these people were the ones who made sure he sat in that gymnasium on that day. They financed and coached him; Downing dropped him off and would take him home.

The hum of whispered conversations ended as the moderator and his three observers stood before the students. They laid out the rules for taking the SAT and what the students could expect. Shortly thereafter, with answer sheets distributed, the first part started.

Jason did not use his abilities to steal any answers from anyone. The questions posed no challenge.

✢   ✢   ✢

After stepping off the school bus on the following Monday afternoon, Jason went directly to the kitchen. As he poured a glass of Kool-Aid, he noted the opened envelope on the kitchen table with his name on it. The scribbled note on the envelope surprised him.

> *Jason,*
>> *We need to talk. I cannot think of any reason to stop you from pursuing this. Let's work together to see how I can be of help.*
>>>   *Frank.*

Jason pulled out the folded sheet. He noted Lipton's name at the bottom and then read:

> *Mr. Sutter,*
>> *I will be attending a professional conference in the coming month of May in Poughkeepsie, NY. I intend to visit Elizabeth Sutter in the Poughkeepsie State Hospital during that week. Since I believe that this is the same Elizabeth Sutter noted on your birth certificate, I extend an invitation for you to join me. If you are agreeable to this plan, please contact me, and I will provide the details. All traveling costs will be covered by myself.*
>>>   *Sincerely,*
>>>   *Hiram Lipton, MD*

Jason fell into a chair, his hand on his forehead. The biggest obstacle to reaching his goal, standing by his mother's side, had evaporated from his path as if by magic. He stared this gift horse in the mouth and wondered why it was all working out so well. Fate had played into his hands. Lipton had provided the means, and Frank had promised support. It did not feel real. He wondered what was next.

Jason carefully refolded the note and returned it to its envelope. He made a mental note to talk to Frank. Lipton would need an answer soon. Options flew through his mind while the envelope in his right hand tapped on the table.

"Before Christmas for Dr. Lipton," Jason whispered. "My SAT scores after." Christmas held the middle, and he hoped it would be a good one.

Christmas was in the frigid air. Frank pulled a team of kids together, and they searched and found strings of lights in the basement. For the first time in years, the old Victorian house lit up the street. The joy of the season radiated from the children, and Frank strung every light they could find.

The toolshed became the focal point for Jason to make sure he left no loose ends. His executive committee to this end included only Russ and Suzy. Their goal was to make sure Jason could leave with all possible outcomes considered. Since Jason had revealed Russ's special nature, like Suzy's, Russ had become more thoughtful; he had matured. Patti's secure and happy life remained his top priority. Russ, however, was one of the loose ends.

"Do you think you should stop hiding Patti?" asked Russ, sitting in his usual place at the workbench.

"I don't think so." Jason stared at the bench surface thinking. His head rested on his finger-entwined hands. "Better safe than sorry at this point." He looked up at his friend. "If everything goes okay with my mom and things are safe, I will lift the memory block."

"Got it." Russ did not argue with Jason anymore on any issue. He stood in awe of what had happened in Kearny. This was no longer a child's comic book with characters either black or white: superheroes or villains. It was family and true friends in a fight where either could be seriously hurt or killed.

"I have tried," said Suzy, "to see the world the way that Bill person saw it." She tried solo meditation to enhance her skills. "I can't do it." Frustrated, it was hard to accept her part as only an energy source.

"Maybe it's a matter of time and need," Jason said. "Like my moving things with my thoughts."

It got quiet. The cold permeated everything in the shed. Suzy pulled her thick, green sweater tighter, flipping the wide collar up to insulate her neck. Russ rested his head on the heel of his hand and, deep in thought, started to pick at splinter imperfections on the bench top with his index finger.

"Do you guys recall that time," said Russ slowly, "the one time you meditated together and things got weird?" Russ wiped the imagined splinters off the bench top with a swipe of his palm and sat up straight. He looked from one to the other. "Remember?"

Jason's eyes locked on Suzy's.

"No secrets. Right?" Suzy said. "Tell him."

"Suzy and I are . . . Well, we think that . . ." Embarrassed, Jason stared at the ceiling corner and then at the cot. He finally took a deep breath and spilled it. "We think we are meant to be together." The confused look on Russ's face pushed Jason to elaborate. "Like your parents, ya know?"

"My parents?" Russ shook his head.

"We will," said Suzy, annoyed by Jason's inability to confront the issue head-on, "in time, become husband and wife like your mom and dad. Probably more like Jason's parents, I would think."

"Oh." Russ rubbed his chin and smiled. Jason groaned on the inside with the expectation of another Russ-improbable idea. His friend surprised him.

"How did you get that when you floated?" Russ looked one to the other. Neither Jason nor Suzy found the words to explain. "I mean, it's going to happen to me. Right? How does it work? Help me out here, guys."

"Okay, Russ." Jason shifted in his seat. He avoided looking at Suzy. "It wasn't like a news report. It was a simple, overwhelming feeling that I didn't want Suzy to ever leave my thoughts. Ever!"

Suzy reached across Russ to put her hand on Jason's. "Yeah," she said, "like that."

Russ stared at Suzy's arm reaching over to Jason and nodded. "I get it. It's kinda like breathing. No one tells you how to do it. Ya just know. Right?"

"Yeah," said Jason and Suzy together.

"Okay, okay." Russ raised his arms, signaling that he was about to make an important point. "If you two floated together and nothing happened to help Suzy with what she could do, and doing it alone makes no difference, why shouldn't Suzy and me give it a try?" Suzy perked up. "I mean, what have we got to lose?"

"Nothing," said Suzy, already off the stool and getting comfortable on the cot. Russ joined her.

"Your turn to be the lookout and take notes, Jason." Russ grinned ear to ear and winked at Suzy. Jason's reservations were overruled before he could express them. Suzy and Russ had decided.

Suzy found her practiced way to a deep meditative state quickly. Russ stumbled along behind her but eventually found his serenity. In that instant, Russ felt Suzy's mind. They became linked: two of a kind. They had no idea what they were doing but jumped into the unknown together.

A wall of buttons, switches, and levers materialized before them. Joyously, with no concerns for the outcome, they pushed every button and threw every switch with abandon. Suzy climbed up on Russ's shoulders to get to the things higher on the panel. She pushed buttons on her way to reaching a bright-red lever. She warned Russ and then leaped and stretched out her hand as far as she could and laughed when she lost her footing and landed on Russ's shoulder. She tumbled with Russ to the ground. The red lever was up instead of down, as it had been. Their universe shifted.

Russ hung over his house with Suzy beside him. They sensed his mother's mild abilities and Patti's hidden brightness. They laughed and tried to see the whole joyous world.

Jason stood outside the toolshed door, considering other issues, when Russ's and Suzy's loud laughter brought him back inside. Russ had tears streaming, which surprised him. Suzy was completely at her ease. She got up and reached for Jason's hand and patted Russ on the back.

"I think I get it, now," Russ choked out. He smiled through his tears. "Just call me Robin, Batman."

Jason's next best thing—after Dr. Lipton's letter—struck in February and March. As if in a tornado, Jason was swept up in sudden notoriety when his perfect SAT scores were reported in February. His whirlwind success became public and pulled in congratulations from all quarters. When the principal announced the achievement to the whole school, Mrs.

Hatcher accused him of cheating, like the cackling, wicked witch flying by Dorothy's window. In March, New York University offered him a full scholarship to study whatever he wished. Frank could not believe it and said he expected Jason to follow that yellow brick road.

"I am not sure how this all happened," said Frank to Jason privately. They sat across the desk from each other in the den, where Jason had long ago discovered the book of maps showing him where Franklin Chase was. "Even Lydia said there was something special about you," Frank said. He shook his head, amazed at this boy he and Lydia had thought so little of and treated so poorly.

"Forget it, Frank." Jason insisted. He felt uncomfortable with his foster father's confession. Frank had no awareness of how he had manipulated Lydia and given Frank the chance to break free of his inner, iron cage.

"I will do what I can," Frank said, leaning forward. "You can help some of these kids follow you after you get settled."

Jason extended his right hand across the desk. "You can count on it."

Frank shook his hand and smiled. He had lost sleep, unable to see how he could help the eight younger kids in his care. Hope had made a late, though awesome and lasting, appearance in the Dubois house.

☆   ☆   ☆

"I am here to tie up a few lose ends before I go," Jason said to Mrs. Hatcher in the teacher's lunchroom at the middle school. A counter beneath the line of windows opposite the door held a hot plate, a large coffee maker like one used in a diner, and lunch supplies: cups, paper plates, sugar, salt and pepper, and other necessaries. Two tables sat along the left wall with four chairs each with napkin dispensers. Hatcher sat at one. A couch and well-padded chairs graced the right side of the room. They were alone.

"I'll have you suspended, Mr. Sutter, if you do not leave immediately." Hatcher was outraged but found she could not move. Jason ignored her.

"You have been a witch in the classroom," Jason said. "You are a singularly terrible teacher. What you do is evil." He walked from the door and sat across from his teacher. "You know that, don't you?"

"How dare you!" she yelled. "Who do you think you are!" She stared at the door, expecting a rescue. Jason smiled at her and waited.

When no one came running to see what the yelling was all about, he shrugged. "I am leaving soon for NYU, but I just can't leave my classmates with someone as awful as you." Jason stood up and went to a window that overlooked the playground. "I will show you who you really are."

"I know very well who I am." Hatcher seethed.

I don't think so.

She pushed back against her chair to get away from her mind's invasion. The movie of her life flashed in her thoughts, with emphasis on key moments pushing her to evil. It came unabated. She could not escape. Myth and fantasy about the good of her family melted away. Only the harsh reality remained.

"Now," said Jason, "you have a choice." He moved from the window and left the room.

Released, Hatcher sat quietly, exhausted, unhurt, but in shock. After a short time she recovered, left the lunchroom, emptied her locker, and met with the principal.

A young substitute teacher taught her afternoon classes. Mrs. Hatcher had taken a sudden sabbatical for medical reasons. The positive effect on Jason's classmates came out as a giant sigh of relief. Jason hoped Mrs. Hatcher would take some positive steps also.

Jason started early to say his good-byes to those closest to him. He expected that leaving Suzy would be most difficult. Artie's feelings, however, took him by surprise. "Man," said Artie at the end of April as they walked to the line of school buses to head home. "I thought we'd, like, be somethin' special at Augustines. Ya know."

Jason kept quiet.

"I mean, it was you and me against Hatcher and sometimes the coach." Artie kicked stones as they walked then stopped. "You and me winning the games for Hoover. You and me, man."

"There's stuff I have to do." Jason felt bad for his friend and decided to tell him part of the story. "I'm going up to New York to get to my mother.

She's in a hospital and she needs me. And I got into New York University."
Jason looked at the line of yellow buses and then back to Artie. "I just got
stuff, ya know."

Artie nodded. "I get that." Slowly he stuck out his hand, and Jason
took it. "Do what you gotta do, but I am going miss you not being there
on the field with me."

They shook. Nothing more could be said.

Artie would transfer to Saint Augustine's starting in the fall. They
would give him a full scholarship after reviewing his test scores. He would
be the only freshman playing with the varsity team.

Jason did what he said he would do. He came out from under his rock
and dug into the history books on slavery in the United States. It was an
ugly story in many parts, but full of amazing courage. The final chapters
had yet to be written from Jason's point of view. The American Civil War
still played out, and even Jason, consumed by his own troubles, heard
of the Freedom Riders and the Klan. He often wondered if he should
intervene. Why weren't the Communities jumping in to maximize justice
in this country, their country? Would they have interfered if a missile
had been fired from Cuba? What would they do if their existence was
threatened? Many questions, no answers.

Chapter 11

Jason stuck his head out of the Mercedes window into a rush of sixty-mile-an-hour wind. He gawked at the gray steel spires of the George Washington Bridge. In the distance he saw the New York City skyline; the Empire State building stood majestic in the early evening sunlight. A barge moved slowly down the Hudson River.

"You never did get into Philadelphia? Did you?" Dr. Lipton asked as Jason ducked his head back in the car.

"No. Never did." Jason imagined New York City as a massive jungle of people, concrete, glass, and steel. There would be much to explore; it was like landing on a different planet. Once over the bridge, they headed east to link with the highway taking them north. The city would have to wait, Jason thought. He rolled up his window, because the roar of the wind made normal conversation impossible.

"So what happened to the nutcase killer?" Lipton asked, bringing him back to the story that had carried them this far. The good doctor never quite achieved a relaxed state of driving confidence but did much better as the story became his focus.

"The police found him huddled under a tree about a quarter-mile from the motel. Whimpering, he went with them without trouble. It seemed his ghosts stopped bothering him when the police were around." Jason's self-satisfied smile went unnoticed by the doctor, who focused on the traffic. "The evidence to convict him of a number of murders was found in his motel room. He'll be out of action indefinitely."

"And Amanda Rice?"

"She starts at the University of Louisville's Medical School in September. She's on her way there now to take a few prerequisite courses over the summer." Jason had changed Amanda's memory of him. He realized that the truth was too distracting for her to focus on herself. If asked, she would describe Jason as a gifted young man who had been a great help in sleuthing the troubles with the homebound elderly in Kearny. It was Sally in her hospital bed who quietly convinced Amanda that she was wasting her time with SeniorHomeAid. She nudged her along to medical school in Kentucky.

"Mrs. Tilghman is doing well?"

Jason turned to the doctor; he wondered if he could read minds. It would not be the last time. "Very well. She's back home working in her garden. SeniorHomeAid made her an offer to join their crew part-time as an adviser and counselor to people with whom she grew up. She could be a great help, I think." Jason mused, hoping he had made the right decision in leaving her knowledge of him untouched. He remembered their last meeting.

"That's twice, Mr. Sutter," she had whispered after the doctor left to check on other patients. "Thank you." She had smiled and put her hand on Jason's, which rested on the bed railing. He had leaned close to hear her words.

"You're welcome." He had put his other hand on top and gave hers a squeeze.

"Will I remember you after you go?" She had seen the signs in Amanda: calm, staring off into space, and quiet. Sally had expected that she would be bouncing off the walls with excitement over this amazing young person. Not listening to their conversation, Amanda had smiled when they turned and looked at her.

"Yes, Sally. You'll know me and what happened. I kinda like the idea. I can visit and not hide from you, ya know?"

"I will be waiting for you to come calling, young man." With those words, the medication the nurse had given her earlier kicked in. She turned over, mumbled a few words, and fell sound asleep.

"What about the teacher who took a leave of absence?" Lipton asked.

"I'm not sure. I lost track of her when she left the school." Jason stared out of the window. "Apparently she was not from the area. Maybe she went back home to sort things out."

"And your cohort on the football field? What happened to him?"

"He's off to St. Augustine's on a full scholarship. He's a smart kid." Jason turned back to Lipton, who nodded.

"Well, we will check into our hotel and then find a restaurant for dinner," said Lipton. He read the sign stating that the Poughkeepsie exit was twenty-two miles away. "Tomorrow, my boy, you will see your mother."

✶　　✶　　✶

"Mr. Sutter! Where are you going?" called Dr. Lipton in a hushed but clearly irritated voice in the lobby of Poughkeepsie State Hospital. "There are the rules and protocol in a hospital. You can't just . . ."

Jason turned slowly, his hand on the door leading to the wards. "The rules, doctor, do not apply." Each word he spoke emphasized that nothing of this Earth could stop him. Jason abandoned the doctor at the front desk. Lipton stared for a moment at the empty space where Jason had stood.

"Of course he would feel this way," Lipton said to himself. "Stupid of me to expect—" He stopped when he realized the receptionist was watching him. "Sorry. It's his mother."

While the doctor dealt with the receptionist and the rules, Jason went directly to Elizabeth Sutter's room, number 303. He was surprised to find her dressed; she wore a navy, sleeveless dress that touched her knees. She lay on her made bed with her arms resting on either side, her body rigid. She was a blonde Snow White, poisoned and waiting for salvation.

Although she was severely weakened, the signals were unmistakable. It was his mother.

As Jason stood over his mother, no tears rolled down cheeks. No weak knees buckled in an avalanche of emotion. The mother-son attachment was not there. This did not surprise him. Even now that he was beside her, he did not recognize her. His father's words from years ago flashed into his consciousness, "Be a good soldier." A job needed doing. Dwelling on what was lost would not help.

Lipton and his guide, a fellow psychiatrist, found Jason sitting next to the bed. His eyes were closed; his hand covered hers. Jason needed them to move on.

"Elizabeth is robot-like," said Lipton's escort. "She can be led about for exercise. If we put a spoon to her mouth, she will eat. She does well with a set, daily schedule for visiting the bathroom. Other than that, there is no reaction. It aligns with no known catatonia reported."

Though they were intent on discussing the case further and giving the young man their best advice, they felt a sudden urge to leave. They did, with the agreement to review the documents associated with the case elsewhere on the ward.

Jason launched into her mind. There was not much left.

Berlin at the end of World War II probably looked better than the landscape Jason entered. It was in bright color, not black and white like in the history books. He moved down a street with half-destroyed buildings, kitchen appliances dangling over the edges of collapsed floors, and empty lots of piled debris. The sky was bright blue. Jason walked down the center of an asphalt street with open manholes, their covers upside down here and there. Burned out cars partially blocked his way. The street fell off in places to large pits, where huge explosions had sent that part skyward. In this destroyed environment, Jason felt his mother everywhere and nowhere; he could not pinpoint where she was. The real world kept her body, but finding her mind would be more difficult. He walked on.

After what felt like hours, Jason sat on a concrete block, part of a larger pile of rubble. He looked out on the desolation. To his left and right were the usual bombed-out buildings with some walls still standing. The search's repeating scenes of destruction had wearied him.

"Elizabeth, where are you?" he whispered. The words broke the tomb-like silence. The upset balance pressed for quiet. He fought it.

"Mom!" he yelled at the top of his voice. The push-back almost knocked him over, as if the world had squeezed together and released. Out of the deathly quiet came a sound. Jason remembered hearing helicopters overhead from time to time in Franklin Chase. Were helicopters coming? The sound grew louder.

Across the street from where he sat, two slabs of concrete flooring leaned against each other, forming an upside-down V. The apex was four feet from the ground. The rumbling sound grew louder.

"Stupid boy!" The voice dragged Jason's sight from the sky, where he saw a spiderlike creature barely visible beneath the concrete slabs across the street. Its two thin arms and two legs looked double-jointed. Bent at odd angles, they attached to an emaciated body roughly the size of a human. The large head wrapped in rag strips looked like a mummy. The spider-thing disappeared so fast Jason wondered if he had imagined it and the voice.

"Hide, fool! They're coming." It was a guttural call to action: animallike, desperate.

Jason ignored the copter sound and paid attention to the wasted being in the rubble. He stood up and walked by a burned-out hulk of a pickup truck and then hesitated. The cave-like space formed by the collapsed floor looked like a trap. A clawed hand appeared against the light-gray of the concrete roof. Another beckoned furiously. The head and body clung to the shadows. Jason approached cautiously.

"Hurry, boy!" the voice insisted. "Hurry! They'll be here!"

Jason stopped and looked up at the sky, wondering what was coming. The creature hissed its disapproval. Jason stood before the stack of destroyed masonry and tried to see the thing. Its claws disappeared. Jason squatted to see what he could in the dark beneath the slabs. The whomp, whomp, whomp of blades sliced the air directly above him. He looked up. A hand reached out, grabbed his arm, and with surprising strength, dragged him over the ground and into the darkness.

"Stupid, stupid . . . stupid! They see you. They hurt you. Stupid!" A shadow moved on all fours—all elbows and knees. The sound of the whirring blades above suddenly ended. The damaged person—it was clear close up that this was a human being—crawled to the edge of the entrance and dared a quick look. The dim light showed it to be covered head to foot with a ragged coat and worn, skintight pants. It looked back into the cave at Jason; only the eyes were visible. In that instant, the bond was made. Jason had found what was left of his mother.

Elizabeth Sutter shuddered and tore out of the cave as fast as her spindly arms and legs could push-pull her to safety. Before Jason could get out in the open, she had vanished.

In the hotel that night Jason listened to Lipton snore on the second twin bed while his mind raced. The bathroom light behind the half-closed door acted as a night light. Jason had his hands behind his head and stared at the white ceiling as the entire sequence of events in the lost land of his mother's mind replayed. There was no time to cry or allow emotion to get in the way. He had to be tough, undaunted.

A particularly loud snort caught Jason's attention. The good doctor woke enough that he looked around briefly, like he had no idea where he was, turned on his side, and then closed his eyes. Jason sat up. He watched his friend drop into a deeper, quieter sleep. Circumstances with his mom had forced a decision.

"I need your experience, doctor," he whispered. He collapsed back on the bed, and sleep quickly approached. He yawned. "Maybe it's time you knew the whole story."

Hiram Lipton, like Chiang Chen, was a practical scientist. Chiang focused on agriculture; Hiram made a study of mental illness. The facts had to add up with few if any loose ends. In Lipton's chosen field, incomplete and misinterpreted data drove him. Loose ends abound where human behavior was concerned.

"I see." The doctor sat back on the vinyl-covered booth, frowning at Jason over their breakfast plates in a diner close to the hospital. He drank from his coffee mug and then set it down. "You are telling me that you actually do hear voices but only if you want to do so? You plant suggestions at will? Memory manipulation is a small thing that you can do?"

"Yes." Anxious, Jason studied his doctor's reaction, hoping he had not made a mistake telling him. "I have recently learned how to move objects with my thoughts. I'm not that good at it, but I can do it."

"I see."

"That explains why I'm not in your books and got better when I wasn't supposed to."

The unspoken whispers begging for trust went silent as the doctor's healthy skepticism showed on his face. "Jason, there is nothing that makes sense relative to your case. I agree with your comment, but . . ." Lipton shrugged. The fork in the fingers of his right hand, palm up, moved back and forth as if looking for a logical way to go.

"I see," said Jason. He flopped back on the bench, disappointed. "Where is your pipe?"

"What . . . my pipe?" Lipton's eyes widened as his jacket pocket rose above the table. The pipe spun out next to his breakfast plate. He stared at the pipe as it hopped around the table. A chill like a thousand needles struck him head to foot.

"Hiram," said his long-dead mother, sitting opposite him. "Sometimes you just have to believe." She looked as she did on her hospital bed near the end. Braided silver hair lay over her shoulder. The power of her honest, loving eyes always affected her son. Those eyes looked back at him now. His mother dissolved like a sidewalk chalk drawing in the rain. Jason took her place, but the same honest eyes stayed behind. Lipton coughed as he controlled his strong feelings for his mother. He had not thought about her in a long time.

"I'm sorry." Jason confronted Lipton's saddened gaze. "You wanted proof. I've provided it."

Lipton cleared his throat and then turned away. Slowly, watching the street traffic, he said, "It was she who stood up to my father when I wanted to go against his wishes." A sip of coffee from his cup helped him to calm. "I wanted medicine. He wanted a rabbi." He smiled. "She settled the debate." He turned from the window and looked at Jason. "I haven't thought of her for a while."

They sat in silence.

Then Lipton frowned. "I must tell you, I feel betrayed." He sighed. "Violated."

"But I—" Jason stopped when the doctor raised his hand.

"You did it so easily. I must assume that you have done this before to other people." His tight-lipped frown deepened.

"Yes." Hurt by his friend's inability to accept his story, Jason felt doubly upset with the criticism. "My foster mother tried to use me for some bad purposes. Things she didn't want to remember I forced her to see. It ended her efforts to control me."

Lipton nodded and then said, "They remembered what you did like I know what you just did to me?"

Jason looked away. He watched people climbing out of their booths—laughing, stacking bills on the table to cover the tab. "No." He faced Lipton. "I erased their memories. It was easier that way." Lipton's challenge angered him. *How dare he judge me*!

Calm replaced Lipton's frown. "Are you considering wiping my mind? As you say it, would be easier, wouldn't it?"

"Yes."

They stared at each other. Jason looked away first. He decided to take no further action against his friend.

"I am going to treat what has happened as a demonstration born of frustration," Lipton said. "I apologize for not accepting your story outright." He reached out and picked up his pipe, studied it for a moment, and then shoved it back in his pocket. "I demand that you request my permission for any intrusion into my mind before you make it."

"Yes." Jason nodded. "I won't do it again."

Lipton extended his hand across the table. Their grasp was firm as they shook. A smile found the doctor's face. A sigh of relief came from Jason.

"How did you know where to look, what to do, and how to do it?" Curiosity overrode all other concerns.

"Simple constructs appear in my mind." Jason filled in the details of what took place in the Dubois house since he got there: the dreams, the demons, and the darkness.

"You have no idea how this works on a cellular or molecular level?" Lipton asked.

"No."

"So that is why you are reading the bio, chem, and genetics texts?" Lipton picked up his fork and ate.

"Yeah, I wanna know." Jason felt a shift in their relationship; he would remember the sting of the criticism. Lipton set limits, and Jason had to respect them. Forgiveness from his friend touched him deeply. A deeper trust grew in his heart for this normal man.

"This knowledge," said Lipton unaware of Jason's thoughts, "changes everything." He put his fork on the plate and pushed it away; then he added more sugar to his coffee and stirred it. "Your story makes sense with your history. It puts to rest my many unanswered questions." The spoon continued to clink against the side of the cup. "You mentioned you had a few concerns to discuss."

Jason described what had happened with his mother. Someone or something had imprisoned and persecuted her. She trusted no one.

"How do I get her to stop and listen?" Jason watched as Lipton set aside the spoon. He pulled his unlit pipe from his pocket and put it in his mouth, holding the bowl while he thought. The sadness brought by the memory of his mother faded. After a moment, the pipe stem left his lips and pointed at Jason.

"Although we like to think of ourselves as something more than animals, we pretty much respond to needs and wants just as they do." The doctor leaned forward. "Tell me what worked for you. When you were ready to run, what stopped you?"

Jason closed his eyes. Chiang Chen had confronted him about his abilities based on the idea of plants that were not supposed to grow, but did. Jason was ready to dash away from Chiang, but he wound up at Mrs. Lim's kitchen table.

"Food." Jason opened his eyes and looked into the doctor's.

"That would be a common-sense approach."

The waitress came over and asked if either wanted anything more. She put the check on the table when both said they were fine. Doctor Lipton put money down and slid out of the booth. Jason followed.

"I doubt it is that simple," the doctor said. "There are always complications and subtleties where the mind is concerned." Over the roof of the Mercedes, as he opened the door, he asked, "I assume that you are actually sharing her reality in her mind when you are doing whatever you do?"

"Do you know of another way?" asked Jason.

Lipton laughed as he climbed behind the wheel. Then he reached over to unlock Jason's door. The engine rumbled to life. He turned to Jason.

"Touché."

Chapter 12

A male voice called his name. The man spoke as if he stood next to him. From a meditation position, back ramrod straight with legs crossed beneath him, Jason jumped up and ran for his life. The bushes surrounding him tore at his clothes. He dashed across the north edge of the Great Lawn in New York City's Central Park. He headed east, keeping to paved paths, and exited the park at a full run at Ninety-Sixth Street. Drivers on Fifth Avenue honked their horns and yelled as a stupid kid dodged through the traffic.

Jason did not stop until he hit York Avenue. The East River was the next avenue further east. He stood in the shadow of an apartment building's front door, breathing hard and waiting to see if there was any pursuit. Minutes passed; the street remained empty.

Jason moved from his hiding place and walked at a normal pace toward downtown. He had been in New York City for two weeks. Lipton had dropped him off with the family Kyle Downing had arranged to care for him while he studied at NYU. His chaperons were physicians who lived near Washington Square Park. Jason could easily walk to class from their Twelfth Street walk-up. They provided the rundown on the dangerous and safe parts of the city and then left Jason free to explore.

Checking over his shoulder, Jason turned west at Seventy-Second Street. The late-morning sun graced the street. The valley of buildings glowed pleasantly; car horns blasted in the distance. The traffic lights changed in a sequence as far as Jason could see. He walked slower, taking time to think. Who had found him in the park and gotten so close? Had he underestimated the danger of living in the enemy's camp? He had to be more careful.

Jason's mother, so sure of her reality in the demolished world, had been brought only so far with the promise of food. Lipton's further suggestions had improved matters, but she still failed to trust her son.

"You will be leaving soon," said Lipton over dinner. "You need to be able to find her from a great distance. Is that something that can be done?" The doctor sipped his glass of red wine.

"Sure," said Jason, lowering his forkful of food. He had easily connected with his mother from the diner after the huge, well-muscled, white-clad orderly ordered them out of the room so the patient and the room could be cleaned up. He told them to come back after lunch.

On the drive to New York City, Jason maintained limited contact with his mother to prove to the doctor it could be done. Nothing would be left to chance, and Jason did it. When the car hit the city's streets after crossing the Tappan Zee Bridge, the boy was unconscious. Lipton noted the time and drove around until Jason awoke. He reported that it took twenty minutes for him to recover.

"All of your contacts with your mother must be performed from your bedroom for safety's sake," Lipton warned. "Be judicious if you think you might collapse after a session with your mother."

"I steal energy from anyone nearby," Jason explained. "I didn't this time."

"Steal?"

"Take without permission. I usually spread the pull over many people, so they don't notice." Jason did not feel a need to apologize for the energy thefts.

"Interesting." The doctor turned onto Fifth Avenue toward Greenwich Village. "Alone you have limitations."

It became warmer as Jason reached Third Avenue and turned downtown. At Bloomingdales he went into the department store to enjoy the air-conditioning. He took his time and browsed the store. In the menswear department, he wondered if he should not enhance the clothing Frank had purchased for him. The jeans and shirts struck him as not enough, based on the way people were dressed on the street.

His hand slid over the sleeves of dozens of suits hanging in a recess along the wall. Jason stopped to check the price and to feel the silk lining. The cost of a three-piece suit shocked him.

Huge, strong arms grabbed Jason from behind and lifted him off his feet. Before he could register what was happening, he was carried kicking into a changing room. The door closed with a definitive thunk.

"Now, Jason Sutter, I can either knock you out and tie you up or . . ." The arms around his chest were making it impossible to breathe. "You can cooperate and we can have a nice conversation about you, your mother, and your father." The pressure eased.

"My father?" The irresistible arms released him, and he fell to the floor. Jason turned quickly and looked into the saddest eyes he had ever seen.

The barrel of a man with massive arms said, "Robert Sutter told me you would not know me."

The man had close-cropped, dark hair and wore black slacks with sky-blue, short-sleeved shirt. Jason recognized the orderly from the Poughkeepsie State Hospital. "You," was all he could say.

"Seth." The huge man spoke quietly.

"Okay." Jason stood and studied the stranger. "What about my father and mother?" He tried to read Seth's mind. The attempt failed.

"My mother and I have been looking after you and your family most of our lives."

"Your mother?" asked Jason. The second, more forceful attempt to get into Seth's thoughts met an irresistible block.

"Yes, Sarah Stiles." Seth smiled. "She is waiting for us close by." Seth raised his hand, indicating someplace beyond the closed door.

"What about my father? Is he still alive?"

"Robert and Elizabeth made it so my mother and I could move undetected." Seth pointed to the door. "Let's go to my mother, and we can tell you all that we know."

Jason turned and opened the door without speaking; he had a headache from trying to break into the big guy's mind. Several times in the last hour, Seth could have killed him. Since he still had a pulse, Jason decided he had no choice but to go along.

Seth came from behind Jason and placed a hand on his shoulder. He steered him to the Lexington Avenue doors, and they went downtown in the direction of traffic. Along the way, a woman came out of a shoe store and stayed just behind them.

"The usual place," she said. Then she immediately turned around and moved away. Jason got a view of a tall woman with gray hair pulled back into a bun, disappearing through a doorway.

"The library. The grounds behind the building," said Seth when Jason asked where they were going. Otherwise, it was a silent walk surrounded by the sounds of the city: traffic, whistles, yells, the bang of metal cellar doors after deliveries, and the grind of a garbage truck devouring a load.

In fifteen minutes they passed between the stone lions guarding the halls of knowledge in the New York Public Library and turned right, following the path to the back of the building. It was a large, open space, odd for New York City, with tree and shrub borders on all sides. On a bench reading a book was Seth's mother, Sarah Stiles. Her gray summer dress covered her knees. She looked up as they neared.

"Come sit, Mr. Sutter." Sarah patted the bench's stone surface. "We have much to discuss."

Jason thought her severe looking in a manner similar to Lydia Dubois, but Sarah projected trust and strength. Jason sat. Seth stood where he stopped and put his hands behind his back.

Sarah studied Jason's face carefully and eventually smiled. "My son and I have worked for your family for a long time. We are normal people, but well hidden from your kind by your father and mother as I am sure Seth already informed you." Jason nodded. "Good." She cleared her throat. "We lost track of you when we handed you over to our Pennsylvania supporters, also normal persons. Our job after that was to help Elizabeth, your mother, as best we could."

"My father?"

"We don't know where Robert was taken. We only know that he is probably alive. Someone like him is not thoughtlessly discarded by any Community." She crossed her legs; her hands held a black handbag in her lap. Jason had not noticed it before. "I assume you know your mother's condition." Sarah looked at her son standing guard, and asked. "What can you tell us, and what can we do to help?"

Jason stared at Sarah, then Seth, and finally the ground. "I can't read either of you. How do I know I can trust you?" Jason stared into her eyes, hoping for an easy answer.

"Well, Jason," she said, "sometimes you have to go with your gut." She watched him closely. "We will be disappointed, but if you feel safer going it alone . . . so be it. We will simply stay with Elizabeth, and you will do whatever you need to do."

Jason considered the evidence: Seth as the orderly taking care of his mother and both of them knowing about how he wound up in Pennsylvania. Neither had attacked him in any way. Going it alone, inexperienced, Jason knew, was not going to work.

"Okay, I can't do this by myself. My gut says trust you."

"Good." Sarah and Seth smiled. "Tell us about your mother."

Jason gave her a quick description of Elizabeth's horror and his attempts to make a crack in the fantasy of her reality.

"Here is what I think we need to do." Sarah stood and placed the purse strap over her shoulder. "You need your mother with you. So you must have your own place. You need money quickly."

"How?" Jason rose and followed her. Arm in arm, Sarah and Seth smiled at his naiveté.

"You take it, Mr. Sutter. You simply take it."

✲ ✲ ✲

Samantha Black sat at Rodney Davenport's large desk at the Tarrytown house. She swiveled in the padded executive chair and watched a storm come up from the south. Samantha kept her thick, brown hair short in the summer and dressed Swiss-Army-knife practical. During the summer months, she wore jean cutoffs with extra pockets and running shoes. Men's short-sleeve, army-surplus shirts with button-down pockets with the tails hanging out were her style. These shirts hid a utility belt full of control devices for handling difficult normal people.

The huge disparity in population scared her. Normals outnumbered them two hundred thousand to one and ruled because of it. Hatred seethed through every pore. She believed it should be *her* kind's world.

At five foot six inches with large, almond-shaped, brown eyes, she presented a healthy, twenty-year-old, pixyish exterior, but she possessed the soul of a troll. Samantha would not hesitate to sacrifice her young if it got her higher up in the organization. She was a bully like Rodney but less strategic in her thinking. Fearing only power, her attention went to Community Central's demands. What happened to Rodney would not happen to her.

Tapping her fingertips together, she watched an elderly man walk up the hill from the train platform. Two children ran ahead, and one clung to his hand. He looked down at the child, who obviously said something amusing; his face turned skyward with a hearty laugh.

Samantha knew the normal man; he lived in the neighborhood. She could not remember his name. It was not important. His slow-moving, stooped gate advertised his age. *Sixty or so,* she thought.

"Same as me." Normal people aged so fast, but popped out so many children generation after generation.

Samantha turned, picked a pencil up from the desk, and scanned two ledgers side by side; one was a month older than the other. Their totals did not match. Rodney's last haul had satisfied the needs of all the North American Communities for the year; a tenth of a percent of the total had evaporated over a month. Exactly one hundred thousand dollars had gone missing, and she could not account for it. This made her very uncomfortable. She would not report it to Central until she knew precisely what had happened.

"It makes no sense for a member to steal from the Community." She answered her own implied question. If the issue was not a simple math mistake, a talented, nonmember had absconded with the funds. Samantha tapped the pencil on the ledger as she steadily checked the math. She blew out a frustrated breath after twenty entries and sat back in her chair. Checking the ledgers was futile. She thought maybe it would be best to ignore the small withdrawal. She tossed the pencil on the desk.

"Why make trouble for myself?"

✽   ✽   ✽

"You did what?!" Sarah Stiles was beside herself. The other customers in the deli on Eighth Street, west of Fifth Avenue in Greenwich Village, stared at her sudden outburst.

"I went for a walk along Fifty-Seventh Street." Jason smiled. "I collected images of people from tellers and others in the banks, and guess what?" Sarah frowned. "I ran right into a bank manager working a very large account. He held a good image of the old guy who hurt my friend's sister."

Patti, Russ's sister, had psychic talents that no one in her family realized. Jason had told Russ. And last summer the attack came. Jason had guessed that her uncontrolled mental abilities kicked some demented people into action. The old man's face, the attacker, had stayed with Jason, who had thrown himself in harm's way to protect the little girl.

"I meant," she said through gritted teeth, "for you to take the money from the normal, who cannot track it." She dropped her head in her hands.

"It was a gold mine, Sarah," Jason said, ignoring her horror. "There were at least twenty accounts: a ton of money." Jason jabbed a fork into a big piece of chicken and took a bite. He watched Sarah shake her head; her hands trembled with fear. "Why get all upset? Stealing from the old guy struck me as the right way to go."

"You don't know their leader. He's a demon. Financial details are his life. He will follow the clues right to you and us." She could not look at him for fear she might slap his face.

"No one can trace what I've done." Jason chewed thoughtfully. He particularly enjoyed the garlic dressing on the chicken salad. "Don't worry. I got you and Seth covered." He took a drink from his bottle of Coke.

Sarah Stiles had survived by keeping a healthy paranoia where the Community's capabilities were concerned. She dropped her hands from her face and crossed them on the table. The damage was done.

"How much did you take? Tell me about this old guy." She started eating.

"I took a small amount from all twenty accounts and put the money in an account for Seth Enterprises." Sarah smiled. "We now have access to about one hundred thousand dollars." She nodded.

"The old guy is gray haired, thin, kinda big nose." He stopped eating and thought a moment. "He has a power in his eyes." He continued on the chicken. "They're blue, by the way."

"You are talking about Rodney Davenport. I met him once many years ago, before the troubles." She sat back. "He is the one who attacked your mother in the final safe house. He is the head of the Northeast Community."

Jason sagged in his chair. His anger flared. The fork stabbed into food on the plate and stood upright as his fist slammed into the wall. Sarah jumped at the unexpected eruption of emotion. Up to that point, she had found Elizabeth's son to be without feeling, but something went missing in the boy.

"All I can say," said Jason through clenched teeth, "is that his time is coming."

The moment of fury passed as quickly as it had erupted. Jason resumed eating and then said, "Getting the money was a piece a cake." He tried to reassure Sarah, who stared at him as if he were completely insane. He placed his hand on hers. "Don't worry. I covered my trail, like using branches to erase footprints in the dirt." He paused. "So to speak."

"I pray, young man, that you know what you're doing." She pulled her hand out from under his and glared at him. "You may not feel as strongly as I do about your mother and father, but remember . . . these are the men and women that took down the two of them."

"Yes," said Jason irritated. "They hit the obvious targets but completely missed you, Seth, and me." He glared at Sarah. "They are not infallible. They make mistakes out of arrogance in a belief they wield absolute power."

Jason recalled when Chiang and Downing had made the same point about the enemies they faced in their wars.

Sarah stared at this child. Power beyond her comprehension, like that of their worst enemies, sat across from her. He sounded like a general surveying a battleground while disconnected from the troops doing the fighting and dying.

"Relax and remember. We are invisible to them." Jason smiled, picked up his fork, and twirled a piece of chicken in the tangy sauce. Then he devoured it.

"We cannot be found by those people. I agree, but . . ." Sarah gathered her thoughts while considering Jason. "I worry that in the end it will be you who may not be visible to your mother or anyone else."

In an instant, Jason's mood fell into sadness. He recalled standing at the foot of his mother's bed in the hospital. Something was missing. It gnawed at him. She could not see that he was seeking her.

"Mrs. Stiles," he said, "this is war. I guess it's my turn to fight." Jason could not say the lack of feeling for his mother was a bad thing. That reality would allow extra choices when dealing with a vicious enemy. He didn't have to care; the bad guys could not use his mother against him.

"We are going to win."

Chapter 13

Elizabeth Sutter vanished from the Poughkeepsie State Hospital two weeks later. Seth cradled her in his arms as he left the ward late at night. Jason controlled the people and arranged thoughts in normal people's minds for miles around. Elizabeth would not be missed for long.

Sarah waited in the specialized van they had purchased with the money stolen from the Community. The drive to the city was uneventful.

Jason had taken over the third and fourth of a failed clothing factory. The raw wood floors were scrubbed and stained mahogany, the walls washed, and the windows cleaned. Jason insisted only that a spiral stairway be added to connect the two floors, so they could avoid using the industrial elevator.

The landlord could not believe his luck. A rube from the sticks was willing to pay two thousand dollars a month per floor and sign a multiyear lease. And they happily threw in new kitchen appliances, updated the plumbing, and added higher-current electric wiring to handle the air-conditioning.

Jason's new home was on Thirty-Third Street, just west of Seventh Avenue. He lived on the third floor. His mother, in a special, hospital bed, was on the floor above. Sarah and Seth slept close to her. Clotheslines strung here and there with paisley sheets as curtains defined their private space.

Jason often sat by his mother and read books; investment was his reading passion. Occasionally he needed to think about what he had learned and closed the book; his eyes fixed on the cloth walls, which rolled and moved with the patterns of dark and bright colors. He wondered what he would find behind the curtains. Was Seth tidy, or did he pick things up only when he needed them? He smiled thinking he would have to find out and then went back to his studies, forgetting the question until the next time he sat reading by his mother.

After completing five books on investment strategies, Jason remanded half of the remaining funds to stock and bond instruments that paid dividends. He found the place with the pillars that he had seen in Davenport's mind: the New York Stock Exchange. He realized that unending wealth presented itself to someone with his abilities. The game—how normal cheated or misled normal—was the key to easy money.

Always a quick learner, Jason met and talked with market agents; they chuckled at the questions from the dumb kid. They explained the reasoning openly and in detail, because the boy seemed to be no threat. Jason learned the common-sense money manipulation behind the Community accounts he raided. Yet there was so much more. He shopped the money around and profited with each buy-sell order.

With complete seriousness one evening, he turned to Seth and asked, "Do you think a million would be enough, or do we need a billion?"

Jason floated at the foot of Elizabeth's bed, easily sharing her reality.

Elizabeth Sutter came out from behind the gray slabs forming her cave to investigate the plate of spaghetti and meatballs sitting on a table of debris a few feet from the opening. Jason's patience had worn thin; her recovery was taking too long. Time, the trickster, not the healer, stoked his fear that her reintroduction to reality was blocked. As always, Jason waited in the same place in the usual nonthreatening pose. He leaned on the hulk of a burned-out pickup truck. In painful slow motion, the ragged creature on all fours crawled into the sunlight. She suddenly grabbed the plate with scabbed fingers and tried to escape with it into the cool, safe darkness of her shelter. The plate would not be moved. If she wanted it, she had to eat it while her frustrated son watched. Jason had added this twist several visits back to keep her in view.

The creature, resigned to her fate, knelt by the debris as if in prayer. She unwrapped the mummy rags from her face and furiously shoveled food into her mouth. Lipton's recommendations had been applied. They caused no improvements in her condition except in her willingness to eat in the open. An obvious truth eluded him. He stared off into the distance, thinking.

"I am part of her reality, but her world is an illusion." Jason pushed off the truck, put his hands in his pockets, and moved small bits of rubble around with his foot. "Is this a healing reality of her own concoction or an enemy-controlled reality she cannot escape?" He thought of paisley sheets and swirling patterns tricking the eye.

Jason pulled himself up on the burned fender and crossed his legs beneath him. The only thing he knew to do was meditate, to change the parameters. The curtain might open and show his mother's true reality. With his eyes closed to the rubble world, a connection upward with his floating self by his mother's bed presented itself. Another way down to an abyssal darkness dropped like a released trapdoor before him. He balanced on a cliff's edge. Frightened, but with no choice if he wanted his mother back, he chose downward and leaned toward the unknown. The long fall into total blackness overwhelmed him.

✵   ✵   ✵

Samantha Black had hated the classic 1930s decorations in the office in the Empire State Building. She replaced the heavy oak desk and filing cabinets with efficient metal options. The light-blocking curtains became Venetian blinds. The walls sported replicas of modern art; she trashed the dark, brooding seventeenth-century reproductions. The sleek, black touch-tone phone replaced the old rotary. Modern lighting fixtures chased the shadows away from every corner as she worked into the night.

When at the office, she compromised and wore white blouses with flowing linen pants with pockets. Her utilities for fending off normal people she stowed in the large, black purse that matched her leather, low-heeled shoes.

For three hours she studied a thick file on Community business. He may not have shown the proper respect for Community leadership, but Rodney respected process and organization. He kept meticulous records and notes on using the normals' financial system.

When the telephone rang, Samantha let it ring. Finally, when finished with the current page, she slowly lifted the receiver from its cradle.

"Yes." Samantha's eye remained on the paper.

"This is Jeff in the surveillance office downtown." The voice trembled slightly.

Samantha waited and then looked up. She did not know a Jeff.

"We have a situation."

"Yes." She picked up the next page; she hoped he would get to the point.

"One of our people is out of commission." That got her full attention.

"Jeff." The soft threat reached through the lines. "Be precise. What happened? Was anyone lost?"

"Two hours ago Chester had a seizure. Bit through his tongue. The blood . . ."

"Who?" She cut him off. She did not care about Chester.

"Elizabeth Sutter."

"You followed up?" Samantha was an instant away from slamming down the phone and confronting this Jeff in person. Her fisted hand gave an insistent pounding to the stack of files.

"She's disappeared from the hospital, from the records, the normal minds, from everything we can check."

"Is Rodney still in view?" She held her breath.

"Rodney?" He paused a second, surprised. "Yeah, Rodney is where we left him."

She breathed again. "When Chester is able to communicate, grill him on all that happened and report back to me at this number." She sat back in the chair. "Jeff?" she asked sweetly. "I do not have to tell you that the sooner we have a complete picture, the better we can settle the issue."

"Un . . ." He swallowed. "Understood."

Samantha placed the handset in place and slapped the desk hard. Reena would have to be informed, and it was always dangerous to bring her bad news. Samantha could not ignore the missing money after this. She would scrape the inside of every skull in the bank office, if necessary. Find the trail; find all the usurpers. It did not occur to her that one mind could have stirred up all the trouble.

⁜   ⁜   ⁜

Jason never meant to hurt anyone. Discussing the killing with his mother, Sarah, or Seth was out of the question. He wished desperately that it had not happened. Maybe Suzy and Russ would listen to him, but they and the old shed in the backyard were far away. He shook his head, trying to erase the familiar, sinking feeling; he had felt the same when Frank's mother passed away. It wasn't his fault, but he might have stopped it if he had been more careful. This time his action had destroyed a person.

"Why didn't you just let go?" he chided himself alone in the kitchen. Jason stood, his head down, his hands spread on either side on the counter.

When Jason threw himself into the darkness, the curtain opened on the truth of his mother's tortured imprisonment. In a space filled with storm clouds and sudden blinding flashes, his limp, rag doll, puppet mother dangled with a thousand bright strings flowing from her to a glowing orb in the distance. Her ashen face in a frozen scream horrified Jason. The fibers demanded breaking.

With no clear strategy, Jason became the shield, like when he protected Patti. His sense of self changed. An awareness of great power filled him. What he perceived as his body became a pulsing ball of light: an energy that mirrored and matched the orb.

Jason positioned himself behind his mother; the fibers from her passed through him. The strings coming from his mother into his energy sphere darkened. Those passing to the distant orb started to go dark out in front of him. When Jason pressed harder to accelerate the process, the push back came. The pulses of light came down the lines and recovered ground.

"You can't have her anymore!" Energy from the real world, pulled from any person close to his home, surged into Jason; he struck back with passion. The dark disconnection to his mom overwhelmed the light. Slowly at first, then like a weakened dam that fails in an instant under great water pressure, all resistance ended; the dark in the strings surged to the orb.

Jason failed to stop when the orb blacked out. More energy coursed through him to a distant target. His fury knew no bounds. He stopped only when the power failed and exhaustion hit him. His onslaught stopped.

He dropped to the floor at the foot of his mother's bed and fell unconscious. Sarah and Seth on the nearby couch shared his condition and slept soundly.

"It was like a lightning strike," Jason said hours later. "Then blocks of city lights go out." Jason faced a recovered Sarah and Seth. His tormented soul could not wait for Russ or Suzy. "I may have hurt or killed someone."

"Good for you, after what they did to your family." Sarah smiled and patted him on the shoulder. Jason felt her pride in him.

Seth grasped Jason's problem. "You freed her mind. You did what needed doing to achieve that goal. You didn't want what happened, but it did for a very good reason." Seth put a hand on Jason's shoulder. "I doubt we will have much time, so we have to help Elizabeth get strong as quickly as we can. She's unconscious now, and I don't know when she will come around, but there's no time for self-doubt." Seth dropped his hand.

"I—" started Jason.

Sarah walked up to him, gave him a hug, and said, "Why is it that only we, who strive always to do the right thing, wind up the victims?" She released him and stood back. "Today those who want to keep us in chains had to sacrifice."

Jason did not argue. Neither Seth nor Sarah would understand his sense of failure. But when his mother's smile beamed at him, all self-loathing evaporated. He focused his efforts on her physical healing and psychic restoration.

Back in the kitchen, Jason's head lightly bouncing on a cupboard door. He would not let his ending the life of another person become "no big deal." He felt like a bull in a china shop. He simply did not know what he was doing. How would he learn when a gentle push would suffice instead of a howitzer blast?

"There has got to be a better way."

✻ ✻ ✻

Early Sunday morning, Jason crossed Houston Street at Second Avenue. The Lower East Side of Manhattan lived up to its reputation as New York's infamous Bowery. Scraps of decaying food littered the sidewalk. The closed businesses protected their wares with thick metal gates secured by huge steel locks or with sectioned doors that pulled down like a garage door. The streets looked and smelled bad—the exact opposite of midtown, where the banks resided.

That morning Jason followed a trail he had picked up when he saved his mother. Elizabeth's jailor had faced the full fury of the break for freedom. As the jailor's consciousness melted, images of the old guy—the one named Rodney—had flashed in Jason's thoughts: a cardboard home, bottles of brown liquid, layers of ragged clothes, dangling street signs, and other images of destitution.

Jason turned downtown. A psychic scent pulled him along into a long alley. Bodies, mostly men, snored with mouths open. They cradled bottles. Innumerable flies hummed about the green dumpsters and the lines of rusting garbage cans full of soggy, brown bags of waste. The smell of decay mixed with urine, cheap alcohol, and human sweat drifted into his face, making breathing painful, like smoke from a campfire. He ignored it.

Jason searched every visible face as if he were a dutiful son looking for his wounded father in a Civil War hospital. On a bed of collapsed cardboard, he found Rodney. Jason approached and leaned in close. "Hey! Old guy!" He grabbed his shoulder and shook. "Hey! Wake up!" He lightly slapped Rodney's face. In a rush of spit, a great cough, and arms raised in defense, he opened his eyes. An empty bottle rolled off the makeshift cot and clattered unbroken over the cobblestones.

"Don' hurt me!" the bum whined.

"What's your name?" Jason yelled. The old man lay back, stunned by the question. It took time for him to call up the memory.

"Norman," he sighed and closed his eyes. "I'm Norman."

Hours later, Norman slept on a cot in the corner of Jason's third-floor apartment. Seth had carried the man to the van. Together they had cleaned him up, made easier by his alcohol-induced stupor.

"You're sure about this?" Seth looked at their new tenant while he dried his hands on a red-checked kitchen towel. He had sprayed a can of room deodorizer throughout the space.

"No doubt about it." Jason studied the old man's face. Even though he had a ragged, gray beard, Jason recognized him.

"Well." Seth put his hands on his hips. "He must have made some very bad decisions to be tossed onto the street." He turned as his mother came up behind them.

"I do not approve of this . . . *thing*," Sarah spit out, "being anywhere near Elizabeth." If looks could kill, Norman would have instantly burst into flame.

Jason said, "If his enemies are the same as ours, we can use him."

"How will he be controlled?" she asked.

"Already done." Jason smiled. He had used a small variation on the fixes he had made to his demented foster mother's mind a year before. "For all intents and purposes, he is a normal person and will remain so."

"Your mother?" Sarah headed for the staircase.

"I will tell her when she is ready to hear it," Jason said commandingly. Sarah nodded and disappeared upstairs.

"Now what?" Seth went into the kitchen and tossed the towel on the counter. Jason followed.

"We wait for consciousness and then have some interesting conversations with our guest."

✵   ✵   ✵

The report about Chester's experience came far later than Samantha demanded. She thought it woefully thin and unhelpful.

"He's dead, Samantha." Jeff received no response. "When we went in to scan his memory, he wasn't breathing. We kept him alive, but his brain hemorrhaged in all areas. It was a mess. There was nothing to do but let him go."

"No minimum-energy memories?" Samantha paced before her desk as far as the telephone cord would allow.

"Lights out. Nothing there to read." Jeff paused. "I haven't seen anything like this since the insurgency."

"So do we have a group of insurgents freeing the worst of the people's enemies?" Sarcasm dripped into her voice. She remembered taking out the enemy during their civil war in this manner.

"I . . . I don't know." He hesitated. Samantha caught it.

"What?"

"Rodney's gone missing too."

"Is any other member of your team dead?" She stopped pacing, lowered the receiver, and tapped it against her hand. She put it back to her ear.

"Different surveillance," Jeff said. "An hourly check on position and self-awareness. It wasn't continuous or heavily linked. He was there, and an hour later, he wasn't." The silence stretched. "You still there, Samantha?"

"Call a leaders meeting for tonight." She rubbed her temples. Her head hurt.

She hung up, and a chill ran up her spine. Events were slipping away from her. Where was Elizabeth Sutter? More important, what great force had killed one of her people?

Chapter 14

"Mr. Jason Sutter," said Rodney too weak to leave his cot. "I am Rodney Davenport, the former head of the Northeast Community, sometimes called the New York Community. We wasted a great deal of effort trying to find you." Rodney smiled. "Never did, obviously."

Jason stared at his hated enemy, but his loathing had evaporated. The reaction confused him; it could be a problem. Jason thought about his mother's condition and what had happened to Russ's sister. "This is just a game to you?"

"To me, to whoever." The old man shrugged. The New York Yankees T-shirt and gray sweat pants with black socks didn't seem fitting on the stylish, capable killer. "But . . ." He looked Jason up and down and then studied Seth standing guard. "You may be the game changer." Clean shaven and able to take care of himself with help, Rodney was surprisingly talkative.

"Don't bother," said Jason, who sensed Rodney's attempt to manipulate Seth. "You do not have access to your abilities. Even if you did, you could not affect us."

"I see." Jason watched wheels in Rodney's mind spin as the old man accepted that he was in the presence of power: an untrained and untried power. "What, then, can I do for you, young man?"

"Talk to me. Tell me about the Communities." Jason grabbed a chair from the dinner table and pulled it up to Rodney's cot.

"That's a tall order." He turned on his side to face Jason. "Allow me to confirm my understanding." Jason nodded. "Your mother completely undid your memory." Another nod. "You know nothing of our people or our unwritten understanding with norman."

"Norman?" asked Jason.

Rodney chuckled. "Slang for normal people."

"Oh." Jason rubbed his hands together and then leaned closer to his prisoner. "You said your name was Norman when we found you."

"Ha!" Rodney choked, and he laughed unabashedly. Then he said, "A little joke added by Reena Sorenson." When there was no reaction, he added, "The leader of all the Communities."

"I see." Jason recalled the last name. "I sent her husband home when I met him in Pennsylvania."

Rodney's jaw dropped.

"You know that Bill Sorenson is what we would call a psychic force of nature?" He stared at Jason. "If you did what you said, I will have to recalculate my position."

Jason grinned, sensing that Rodney always worked things out so he would land on his feet.

"What do you know of us not-normal people?" Rodney asked.

"I don't know anything." Jason sat back. He read this old guy like a book, and the old man knew it.

"I can assume since you have me that you also are keeping your mother safe nearby." He looked from Seth to Jason. "She is obviously not able to answer your questions yet, so you came to me."

Jason kept silent. Seth looked away. Jason knew that his silence gave Rodney his answer. Elizabeth Sutter lived free of Community control.

"Well, let's start with a little history, shall we?" The wasted, old man raised his head from the pillow and rested it on his bent arm.

"Yes. Start where you like. We have all the time in the world." Jason looked over at Seth. "I believe we are okay here." Jason controlled Rodney and his abilities completely. "Stay if you are interested."

"I'll stay," said Seth as he pulled up another chair. "I want to hear this."

"You've been living among the normals as if you were one of them," Rodney said. "So you have been confronted with their desire for wealth and control." Rodney pushed himself up further and sat with his legs crossed. "Ever hear of Jesus?"

"Yeah, sure. He's a big deal." Mrs. Hatcher had made a point of noting Jason's lack of religious training. She considered him a soul in dire need of saving from hellfire, so she harped about the unredeemed at least once a week. On those days, she made Jason read many pages from the Old Testament.

"We do not have any written records, which is strange." Rodney stared blindly, considering that strangeness, and then said, "Those that kept records probably got crushed by norman, probably revealed themselves." He shrugged. "I believe that Jesus may have been one of us."

"What?" Jason said, shocked.

"Tell me, young sir, have you performed anything that might be considered a miracle?" Rodney leaned forward and wagged his finger at him when Jason did not respond. "You see what I mean?"

Jason could not argue. He relived Sally falling to the floor and his bringing her back like Lazarus. Suddenly he picked up on Rodney's thoughts. His arrogant prisoner had misunderstood his reaction. Rodney's thoughts about what he would do with "this child" if ever he was free came to Jason. He let them pass without comment. It was obvious who controlled this arena.

"If he was," continued Rodney, "then planting the whole crucifixion story would have been a piece of cake in those times of small populations packed close together. For all we know, he might have decided after leaving Palestine to be a Roman emperor, just for laughs."

"You're guessing."

"I am. Intriguing idea notwithstanding." The old man placed his hand on his throat. "May I have some water?" Seth provided the drink and returned to his seat, fascinated.

"You know, of course, how few children we have?" He drank and then placed the half-empty glass on the floor. Jason shook his head. "It's why we never took over. At our best we cannot come close to controlling billions of normal people. One man with a gun cannot rob a room with a hundred people if they are determined not to be robbed. There may be a few casualties, but the gunman will always be overrun."

"My best guess based on my century-plus lifetime is that we were chased or annihilated in Asia and Europe until we escaped Oliver Cromwell's government in seventeenth-century England and arrived on these shores." Rodney reached over the cot, picked up the glass, and finished it. He waggled the glass in his hand and looked at Seth. The huge man kept his seat. Rodney frowned. "What's for lunch today, my good sir?"

Seth kept his seat and stared at Davenport.

"No lunch today?" The old man frowned.

"Not for you," Jason said. "Mr. Stiles is not a servant. He is a compatriot."

"I apologize, Mr. Stiles, for my discourteous attitude. You certainly deserve better of me." He nodded at Seth, who returned the acknowledgement.

"Pizza?" Rodney smiled.

"You were saying about escaping Europe?" Jason had not missed the point. *You will live for more than a hundred years.*

"Yes, Cromwell and England. The New World and its forever frontier allowed us to thrive." Rodney's index finger emphasized his point again. "No large population centers. Easily manipulated Indian tribes. No one knew we were around. It was a godsend until the frontier ran out. By that time, of course, we were well entrenched. We knew the game and played it better than norman."

"We are only on this continent?" asked Jason.

"As far as we know."

Jason stood, turned his chair around, and sat, resting his head on his folded arms on the chair back. "Tell me about the war."

Rodney coughed and then looked at Jason. "This subject is a minefield." He paused. "I won't apologize for what was done to your family. I will tell you the truth, which might get me killed."

"I asked you." Jason had no sympathy for Davenport's situation. He gave him no other option but to place the facts before them.

"It was me who attacked and neutralized your mother. Others ended your father's ability to make a difference."

"They killed him?" Jason took deep breaths to control his rising fury.

"No."

Stupid flashed in Jason's mind as he read Rodney. "Why stupid?" Jason's fingers clenched the chair back, white knuckled from his little fingers to his index fingers. Anger boiled within him.

"We do not destroy the best of us," Rodney said. "We reuse what we can. Death and destruction are the last resort. There were too many and we—"

"What was it all about?" Jason said.

"Oh." Rodney glanced to his left, thinking. Slowly he came back to confront Jason. "You will have to decide if the sacrifice, your sacrifice, was worthy of the cause."

"What did they want?" Impatient, he tweaked Rodney's awareness. The old guy's head twitched involuntarily. "No politics, no misleading, and no making your side look better. I can tell."

Rodney massaged the back of his head where Jason's psychic slap landed. "Some wanted a sharing with normal people. They wanted to reveal our existence, share our abilities, share their technology, come to an understanding. Our side viewed such a thing as certain death. A thousand years of history was on our side. We stopped it at all costs."

"Where's my dad?" It had been a war between states of mind, and he wanted to focus on the immediate.

"I don't know."

Jason read his mind; it was the truth.

"Reena knows." Rodney added.

Jason said nothing. He stood and placed his chair back at the table. Seth did the same. When he returned, he stood over the old man.

"Just so we are clear." Jason hovered over him like a judge in a courtroom leaning over to confront a perpetrator. "It was I who freed my mother. I freed you from the Community and continue to make sure they cannot find you. It's me." Rodney looked shriveled; all arrogance drained away. "I stopped you from murdering my friend's sister." Jason paused and let it sink in. "I will help you so long as you are helping us. The moment I sense betrayal in any form, your brain will bleed. Do you understand?"

Rodney nodded repeatedly. Jason captured his final thought: *Oh damn!*

☆   ☆   ☆

In a conference room at the Pierre Hotel, Samantha and her department leaders presented the news of their deteriorating situation to Reena Sorenson and her advisers in Bismarck. She looked out of the window at the Plaza Hotel over the treetops of Central Park.

"Form two strike teams. I will send you extra kinetics to enhance their capabilities. More seers will be sent as well." Reena's voice projected clearly over the speaker connected to the multiline, black telephone. "Do you have a starting point?"

"No." Samantha spoke clearly, forcefully, but she closed her eyes, praying that her extraction was not imminent. "My searcher minding the Sutter woman was killed outright. No afterglow or minimal energy left to find."

"If the quarry is protected in some manner, search efforts will be for naught." It was a male voice, unfamiliar to Samantha. She turned from the window.

"This may be what we are facing," said Samantha, walking to the table. "What do you recommend?"

Reena said, "Rodney is the key." All in the Pierre conference room exchanged looks and nods. She continued. "It is he who will work to undo the extraction. To get back into our good graces, he might send up a flare, so to speak. Be ready for it."

"Understood." Samantha felt great relief that no one in Bismarck had criticized her leadership.

"This will take time." Reena paused. "We need to evaluate all that we have done since Rodney was removed. Special help may be necessary. I will make arrangements, depending on the outcome of these efforts."

Samantha sat up straight, feeling the focus of Community Central leveled directly on her. "It will be done as you order. Thank you, Leader Sorenson."

The call terminated.

Chapter 15

When Elizabeth Sutter gained consciousness a week after Jason freed her from her psychic prison, recognition hit her, and she became an emotional basket case. She clung to Jason. Guilt and shame for what had been necessary overwhelmed her. Inconsolable, her steady flow of tears embarrassed Jason. He knew this woman to be his mother but did not feel what he should. His mother's protection continued to work, but she was invisible to enemies and, in this way, she remained lost to him. Finally she exhausted her tears and slept peacefully. His need to know what happened so long ago would have to wait a few more days.

Days later, Jason took a deep breath and climbed the tight spiral of metal steps.

Elizabeth Sutter sat in a dark-green, vinyl-covered chair. As her son approached, she stopped reading and set aside the book. A smile lit her face, and she raised her arms for a hug. Her damaged little boy, whom she had brought into the world, had to be pulled close. Bear hug barely described the strength of her arms about her only son.

"You are bursting with questions," she whispered in his ear and then released him. Jason stood up, looked around, and then dragged a chair over and sat.

He looked her over. "You are much better."

"You are much taller." The words "since last we met when I wiped your mind" hung in the air between them. Elizabeth placed the book on the floor and stretched out her legs. Forgotten strength was returning to her limbs. She relaxed them and said, "I am walking short distances." Jason nodded.

"I . . ." Jason hesitated. What could he say? This was his mother but a stranger-mother, not quite connected to him.

She took his hand and looked deep into his eyes. "You, Seth, and Sarah must keep the block. You are not finished." Her eyes searched his face, her free hand on his cheek; she blessed him and any future action he might take. "We will have to chance that we will know each other completely in a safer world." No joyous, mother-son tears would be shed—yet.

"Thank you." He squeezed her hand. "I have questions and something we need to discuss, since it directly affects you." Their hands separated. Elizabeth sat back, as did Jason, at a business distance.

"First, your enemy, maybe your worst enemy—"

"Rod Davenport," injected his mother.

"Is now working for us." Jason waited for the untrustworthy, hated-killer argument to begin. "He is a guest downstairs under my control."

Her eyes flashed. She imagined her hands strangling the life out of her torturer. She closed her eyes and said in a constrained voice, "I understand. But . . . no matter how well fettered, the fox still dreams of the hen's taste." She relaxed. "Be very careful."

"I will." Jason had his own reasons for using the man on his cot. He changed the subject. "How do we do what we do—what the normals can't do?"

"We don't know." The implied, "it isn't important" was clear. "I guess you could say we are parasites on their progress. We use what they come up with and create a secret life under their noses." Elizabeth became sad, thinking about the lost opportunities to make their tunnel existence—a hidden life in the dark—into a surface life in a radiant light.

"Okay," Jason said, "let's consider the here and now. The Community knows you and Davenport have disappeared. Maybe one of them was killed in the process. How will they react?"

Elizabeth turned to her son and glared at him. She slowly shook her head. "How did you do that without your partner?" Her question surprised him. "That can't be done without a ready energy source. You have to have your partner with you. Do you have one?"

"I sorta, kinda have one in Franklin Chase." Jason sensed her concern and disbelief in what he described. Embarrassed, Jason could not talk about Suzy. He looked away, a shy smile captive on his face. "I just borrowed energy from Sarah and Seth, and maybe some other normal people over a certain area. No big deal. It was the easiest way to go."

After a guttural sigh, an amazed Elizabeth said, "No! You didn't." The half assertion, half question charged with nuance changed the exchange. "I have never," she said slowly, with emphasis, "known anyone to be able to use normals as sources. Not Rodney, not Reena, not any of us."

Jason shrugged. "I just needed to do some things to make stuff better, so I grabbed what I could." *What is she getting all agitated about*, he wondered. He pictured his ring of supporters below the huge, old oak in the sanctuary back in Franklin Chase, and he suddenly missed them.

"You did that to free me?"

"Yes, of course." Jason sat on his hands and pushed himself off his chair. He looked away from his mother like any annoyed teenager sick of the adult rules limiting what he could and could not do.

"All . . . right," said Elizabeth, staggered by the implications. Fighting the intense impulse to demand more details, she returned to the original question. "In response to one of their team being hurt or killed, they form Search and Destroy squads made up of telepaths, kinetics, and seers."

"What?"

"A seer was what your father was to me. Rodney Davenport and I are telepaths. I don't know any surviving kinetics." She moved to the edge of her seat. After a moment of silence, she said, "Kinetics are best described as normals with the ability for action at a distance: telekinesis."

"What does that mean?" Jason stood up and walked in a circle to stretch his stress-tightened muscles. He was afraid. "Can seers see the future?"

"Kinetics are very talented persons who can move things with their thoughts. They turn objects into killing weapons. They, however, have a limited range and power. They are easily nullified by persons like me or you, as long as there are only a few of them. In large numbers, they overwhelm our abilities. In large numbers we die." She paused and then said, "Our seers are not like the normals' definition of *seer*. They are see-ers. They are able to find our kind."

"What if a telepath can do what a kinetic does?" Jason leaned over the back of his chair.

"No such thing." She stared at Jason, afraid to ask the question sizzling to be spoken.

"Yes." Jason read her urgent question. "I am not sure how good I am at it."

His mother stared at him. The same disbelieving look he had seen from Lipton settled on her face.

"Are you able to search as well?" She tried to stand but did not have the strength to push up her weight. Jason did not try to help her.

"I . . . I don't know." He fixed on Elizabeth's eyes. "But I never tried. If I could . . . what of it?"

She broke contact and turned away. "Then you are something very different."

Jason smiled. He had always been different. Why shouldn't he continue to be so? The coming battle, however, needed discussion. "In your experience," Jason asked, "would they send a few or many kinetics?"

"Probably three or four." Elizabeth collected herself. Her son's nature could be handled later. "Maybe more if they think Davenport is on our side." Elizabeth brought her hands together and folded her fingers together.

She thought and said, "It will take time to put these teams together and into position here."

"How long?" Jason straightened up and started pacing. Elizabeth's eyes followed his every move.

"Weeks, at least."

"So I need to act soon." He closed his eyes, wondering what to do.

Elizabeth held her breath and then released it. Her son faced a dire choice. One mistake would cost all of them their lives. Her heart went out to him. She reached for him to hold his hand. Jason, immobile, stared at the extended hand.

"Go," she said reluctantly. "Talk to Rodney. He can be a great help."

Jason took her hand in both of his. "Thank you."

"You are right." Elizabeth stood, this time without Jason's helped. She threw her arms around his shoulders and whispered, "Go do what you must."

Jason developed a taste for strong, iced coffee over a number of grueling weeks. The caffeine surge allowed him to believe he was a step ahead. He sipped from a tall glass, watching Rodney devour a slice of pizza at the dinner table. Seth sat next to Jason. The big man took small bites, and Jason ate slowly.

Jason opened the conversation. "You are not attached." He paused. "Not married like my mom and dad."

Reluctantly, Rodney pulled his eyes from the pizza box. Seth's hand rested on the lid; he was the gatekeeper to dinner.

"Never found someone I could tolerate for more than a month." Hungry, Rodney pleaded silently with Seth. The big man's fingers drummed on the cardboard.

"Where did you get your power to act?" Jason nodded to Seth, who removed his hand and pushed the box toward Rodney.

"I had a stable of seers available to me at all times." He glanced at Seth. "One or two stayed close day and night." The wrinkled hands lifted the lid. His eyes widened in appreciation of the treasure within.

Jason changed the subject when he realized that Rodney thought Seth was his seer. "Tell me about your replacement."

"Dear, sweet, cutthroat Samantha Black is Sorenson's puppet." Rodney reached in and teased a slice from its sister slices. It dripped olive oil on his paper plate. "She is gifted but has a fatal flaw." He took a big bite, grabbed a napkin from the pile next to the box, and wiped the runoff from his chin. "She acts decisively but does not assess the success of her actions. She makes the same mistakes over and over."

Jason grinned. "What mistakes?"

Rodney provided useful, actionable data on the enemy: "She will execute to Reena's instructions. She will not consider that Reena might be wrong. She will not consider the practical reality on the ground before her. Anything special, like you, Mr. Sutter, will throw any plans into disarray." He smacked his lips, intent on seizing some of the extra cheese, embedded with onion and green pepper, falling from the slice's edge. He quickly raised it higher; the cheese lump fell into his mouth. He slurped the mozzarella cables like a small child slurps sloppy, sauce-covered spaghetti.

Jason found Rodney's nonchalant attitude annoying. Jason wanted him to care about his survival. "What is your assessment of kinetics?" he asked.

"Great at taking out normans." Jason had stopped trying to get him to drop the insult. "Pitiful at working against someone like me . . . or you." Rodney put the slice on his plate, grabbed the can of soda to his right, and finished it. "Aaah. Kinetics are like normans with this extra ability."

"Do they blend in better with normal people."

"You would think they would, but in my experience, they are loud, uncontrolled, and more trouble than they're worth." Another soda hissed as Rodney opened it. He quickly held it away, aiming the spray at Seth, who ignored such small insults. The can failed to shoot its contents.

"How do they blend?" asked Jason.

"First, they drink too much." He tossed the tab onto the table. "Hard liquor." Rodney held the can in his right hand tilted toward Jason. "Their abilities and alcohol are a lethal mix. Kinetics are too much like normans when it comes to alcohol and drugs. You would not believe the number of times we had to clean up after a drunken brawl. Many normals died." He chuckled. "Of course, when kinetics got really stupid drunk and attacked us, we killed them outright. I guess we did them a favor in that way." He drank, keeping his eyes focused on Jason.

The lackadaisical attitude toward murder upset Jason. All he could say was "Oh?"

"We culled the herd of the worst offenders." Rodney put the can down and then lifted the pizza from the paper plate. "They are a much less stupid lot now and more manageable." He devoured the half-eaten slice.

"You ever run into one?" Jason turned to Seth, who shook his head. "What did you mean about kinetics being like normal people who use drugs and alcohol?"

"You ever have a drink?" Rodney's left eyebrow rose as he chewed on one side of his mouth.

"Yes, wine. I didn't like it much." Jason recalled Kyle and Mary's wedding reception.

"Of course you didn't." The thin lips smiled. He swallowed. "Tastes like sewer water to us."

"Why?"

"Ha!" laughed the old man. "I have no idea. Just does."

Jason's frustration with the older generation and their ignorance of how things work flared. He stood abruptly with fists clenched at his sides. Seth and Rodney stared at him, confused by his reaction.

"You don't know much, do you?"

"Now, you just listen to me, young man." Rodney started to rise from his seat. "You don't know where you come from."

Suddenly Jason's finger was in Rodney's face. "You don't know how you do what you do or why you live longer than normal folks. You complain and attack normal people, but they can answer those questions. Worst of all, you enjoy killing." Jason collapsed into his seat. He recognized the "yeah, so?" reaction in Rodney. He realized his rant was a waste of time, and his calm returned. "Let's move to another matter. Tell me about their fighting style."

Rodney grinned, the insult forgotten, and wiped his mouth with a fresh napkin. "Are we at war? Will you need me, Mr. Sutter?" A question hid within the question: *Do you need me to be functional*?

"Not yet, Mr. Davenport. I know where your loyalties lie." Jason's fingers lightly touched his glass of iced coffee and turned it in place. "You are loyal to yourself."

Rodney laughed. "Of course, I am," he said, unapologetic.

Seth ate quietly.

Jason's serious, unforgiving glare wiped the grin from the face across the table. Then he said, "As I see it, you have Elizabeth Sutter, growing in strength upstairs and Miss Black ready to end your life if presented with the opportunity."

Rodney suddenly swallowed with difficulty.

"You are a dead man without me." Jason lifted the coffee and drank. The heavy glass hit the table with a bang, and coffee splashed the table. "Don't mess with me. I'm constantly burdened with searching for good reasons to keep you alive." A silence hung in the air. Seth stared at Jason. "Remember," Jason said, "the girl lives. I took your worst blows, yet here I am: alive and well."

Rodney stood unsteadily. "I must apologize. I am an ingrate at the least." He looked at Jason, then at Seth. "Thank you for pulling me from that alley and giving me back my name." He took a deep breath. "I will do all I can to help you. In all honestly, if our positions were reversed, you would be dead." He considered his next words carefully, given the power sitting opposite him. "I am what I am. If the fight goes against you, I cannot say I will be loyal and go down to ignominious defeat or death. Do not trust me to be loyal. Trust me to go with my own self-interest."

Jason climbed to his feet. Seth rose also.

"We cannot ask for better from you, Mr. Davenport," Jason said as he extended his hand across the table. Rodney grasped it, and they shook.

"I expect," said Jason with great emphasis, "you will teach me to be an exceptional telepathic warrior."

Rodney felt sick after the talk over dinner. He folded the blanket around his body and went to his cot. With new data about this boy, he realized he had made the mistake of underestimating him. This was no snot-nosed teenager stumbling around in the world. He had shared a meal with his liberator: someone who obviously worried Reena Sorenson.

Rodney recalled Robert and Elizabeth. When they had finally been cornered in an isolated, rundown farm house near Albany, New York, they had not tried to defend themselves. Sitting side by side in the front room calmly, as if waiting for a taxi, they welcomed their attackers. Robert was used up, he remembered. The man barely kept himself conscious. Elizabeth's energy stores drained slowly. Rodney sensed Elizabeth, but his mind failed to find Robert. Their eerie smiles sent shivers down his spine. He ordered the house checked for traps. None were found.

The Sutters's captors attempted to pry open their minds. They learned nothing about Jason's whereabouts as Robert and Elizabeth crumpled and slid to the floor. Now the boy, their offspring, had sat on the other side of the dinner table with a cold drink and had threatened him with annihilation. Rodney hated feeling powerless.

✻   ✻   ✻

August 15, 1964

Dr. Lipton,

    I am doing well. My mother continues to improve. Your guidance was invaluable. I am excited about starting classes in about three weeks.

    Concerning the odd conditions of which you are fully aware, I have built a life away from the good people you planned for me. They believe I have followed the plan laid out by my friends in Franklin Chase. You know the truth of it.

    My mother is with me with two people who have been with my family for many years. They are a great help. I believe that I will have need of you in New York at some point. I request that you introduce yourself to Kyle and Mary Downing, Louise Deloro, and Professor Chiang Chen. Miss Deloro is Mary Downing's sister. You may have to rely on Kyle Downing to contact Professor Chen. Their knowledge of me is limited now, but was complete a year ago in the summer. They may need some help understanding what has happened here. I hope to bring them back to the same level of understanding that you enjoy.

    You will be contacted by two young persons: Russ Wyatt and Suzy. Suzy lives with Frank Dubois, my former foster parent. They are my kind but have different talents. They are aware of you and your involvement in saving my family. Russ and his family's contact information can be found in the phone book.

    I have provided you with insight into what I am facing. With this in mind, do not keep this note. Destroy it. Please see my new

*address and telephone number. If you have any questions, feel free
to give me a call.*

Sincerely,
Jason Sutter

Blue smoke curled from Hiram Lipton's pipe. He held the letter in his right hand and the pipe in his left. He reread the letter and considered what to do. The pipe went to its holder, and the letter settled on his desk blotter. Lipton stood and studied his shelves of books. The thick phone book slid from the stacks and landed next to the letter on the desk.

Chapter 16

Samantha Black called the first strategic elimination teams to meet in Tarrytown on the first Tuesday night in September. Men and women in small groups sat or stood around the big brown couch. Huddled in the entrance to the huge room, they picked at the leftovers from dinner. Kinetics drank sweating bottles of beer and laughed loud and long; they thrived on brash behavior. The more gifted sipped iced tea or lemonade and enjoyed their friends but kept a discrete distance from the telekinetics.

As the Northeast Community leader, Samantha brought the meeting to order by tapping the side of her tea glass with a spoon. Heads turned; the talking and laughter died. The various groups from the kitchen and hall flowed into the living room like monks called to evening prayers. Samantha put her glass next to a stack of papers. When she scanned the room, she read as many eyes as possible.

"One of our own has been murdered!" She did not need abilities to get the crowd's reaction. "We are here tonight to form the teams and commit ourselves to avenging this heinous crime." Heads nodded.

"To that end, it has been ordered that two kill teams be launched to bring the criminals to justice." Samantha pulled a piece of paper from her shirt pocket. "You have all been given one of these." She shook the paper to make her point. "I will lead one team, and Jeff Thornton will lead the other." She searched the faces in the room. "Jeff, where are you?" A tall, ruggedly handsome, twenty-something male in the back raised his hand.

"Jeff's team will review strategy and actions in the dining room." Samantha lowered her hand holding the list. "My team will stay here." As she folded the paper and stuffed it in her pocket, she said, "Are there any questions before we get started?"

"We haven't been told what we might be facing. What killed your man?" The questioner tilted his beer bottle, keeping a wary eye on Samantha.

"It was a telepath, like me."

The rumbling discontent among the ten kinetics slid around the room. A few voices dared to describe the operation as suicide.

Shut up! flashed in every mind—angry. The room quieted.

"You will be fully supported by seers and telepaths. The enemy will be outnumbered ten to one." Samantha looked the questioner in the face. "It is what Central wants. If you have a problem, take it there." With that threat, the beer-drinking complainers kept their concerns to themselves.

"Samantha?" asked a young woman sitting on the couch. "Do we know the logistics: where they are, who they are, and what they can do?"

"We believe they are on Manhattan Island. We do not know exactly who they are." She hesitated and added, "Rodney Davenport may be working with them." Shock and the whispered, "We don't have enough" hung in the air. They all were too aware of Davenport's history.

"We have reason to believe," said Samantha quickly, "that Rodney is severely weakened from his extraction earlier this year." She raised her hands. "He is not a huge concern."

"Can you see him?" The question came from someone by her opened office door.

"Not at this time," she admitted. Normal humans would have said that you could hear a pin drop in the crowded room. A telepath unprepared for the reaction would collapse under the onslaught.

"Reena Sorenson herself set the plan in place!" she yelled. "Who of you wishes to complain to her?" She stared around the room, and the sudden mental quiet satisfied her. "We are also targeting Elizabeth Sutter, who recently disappeared from our view."

The name Sutter, a known power behind the insurrection, sent a chill among the teams. All in attendance realized something had gone wrong.

It took the skill and strength of a Rodney Davenport to bring down the last people to stand against Central: the Sutter cohort. Now a Sutter and Davenport might be working together? Confidence leaked from the room faster than water from a rusted tin bucket.

"Form your teams and start working the strategy for getting this done." She paused. "Remember, this is a kill mission only. No recycling, no mercy. Kill everyone."

Half of the room emptied, following Jeff to the dining room. Those remaining looked at Samantha, hoping she had a sensible, obviously successful plan.

"We start in Battery Park, with our seers linked together for optimum identification." She handed out sheets of paper prepared earlier and stacked on the side table."

Hours later, the debate-exhausted teams left the house unhappy but committed to the kill order.

Samantha and Jeff commiserated over their teams' fears. Aside from cheerleading, there was nothing else they could do. Jeff left anxious to get back to the office and check on his monitors. Samantha yawned and trudged upstairs to the bedroom she used when at the Tarrytown house. She turned off the lights as she went.

Samantha used the bathroom, and then the footsteps of her bare feet pattered down the hall. The old wooden floors creaked. Samantha collapsed into bed, and the house became as quiet as a graveyard on a still summer night.

Downstairs in the office, a swivel chair groaned slightly. The small desk light switched on, and Jason Sutter, elbows resting on the chair arms, his fingertips touching, considered all that he had heard.

"Not cool, Samantha Black. Not cool at all."

☆   ☆   ☆

"You remember that talk you had with Mr. Davenport on strategy?" Seth always called Rodney "Mr. Davenport." Jason and Seth were working out their moves for the next day over the dinner table. The empty dinner plates lay stacked at the edge of the table.

"Yeah," said Jason, focused on the maps of downtown Manhattan. "I do."

"I remember you got real angry at one point," Seth said as he piled their glasses on top of the plates. "I didn't quite get why you got mad." Jason looked up. "Just thought I'd ask, since we're using his tactics. He is, after all, trying to help."

Jason sat back in his chair and considered his friend and protector. "Seth . . ." He tried to find the right words. "It's all such a letdown."

"How?" Seth hefted the dirty dishes and hauled them into the kitchen.

"The wasted time, the stupidity of it all," Jason yelled, hearing the dishes being placed in the sink and the water running. "I mean, I'm just a kid, and I can't understand it."

"Understand what?" Seth came back to the table wiping his hands on a dish towel.

"How can those of us in the Communities not have found solutions to our problems?" Jason watched Seth's confusion give way to understanding.

"We normals," said Seth following the logic, "found solutions to problems and made progress over the centuries. Your kind didn't. You simply piggybacked on our advances." He nodded at his own analysis. He balled up and tossed the towel onto the counter across the room.

"For example," said Jason, "why don't we understand why we do not have as many children as normal people do—generation to generation. We have seers, telepaths, and kinetics. Why don't we have doctors, nurses, scientists, engineers . . . you name it. It's like we have all this power and that's all there is. We just live with our problems."

"You think it is that simple?" Seth said as he sat down beside Jason.

"Nothing is ever simple. I have learned that lesson." Jason leaned over the table with his hands together, fingers entwined, and said, "I have also learned from the people like me I've met that they never tried. They got lazy or too terrified to try. Either way we will, in time, die out. Maybe, now that I think about it, that is what the war was really all about."

"How so?" Seth studied his young man, his charge.

"Die out fast by taking a risk. Attempt to figure things out with normal people or die out slowly, overwhelmed eventually by the normal population, unable to save ourselves."

"Your dad said something like that to me some years ago, but I didn't get it." Seth stood and walked around to the other side of the table. He pulled the maps around, ready to get back to work. "I got it now."

"Did my dad ever talk about why our kind never tried to stop some of the more dangerous activities of the normals?" Jason thought for a second. He craved any words about his father but feared he would be disappointed. "Ya know, things that might get all of us killed too?"

"Your dad with your mom actually intervened in some small crises, which saved some normals' lives in the early fifties." Seth rubbed his chin, remembering. "Only once though. He said that without all the Communities working together, it would only lead to self-destruction."

"Sounds like what the war was about." Jason felt proud of his parents.

"More or less," said Seth. He went back to studying the maps.

"I'm going to find him, Seth." Jason got up and joined the big man in another review of the plan.

"I know." Seth smiled.

They discussed their movements to combat Samantha Black's killing operation and what to do if things did not go as expected.

"By the way," Seth said as they folded the maps, "you need to register at the college if you intend to start learning about all the things the Community does not care to know."

"Damn, I forgot." Jason had scheduled no time for this trivial action. He had battles to fight.

"We'll find the time." Seth smiled.

✳   ✳   ✳

A teenager in a Yankees baseball cap hung out at the entrance to the Staten Island Ferry. He was a stone's throw away from Battery Park in Lower Manhattan. Fifteen people who looked like tourists gathered at the railing overlooking the harbor. When the ferry blew its horn, the group of fifteen broke up. Ten moved off in all directions. Five held together, moving as a unit. Seth sat on a bench nearby, acting absorbed with the *New York Times*.

Jason, his ball cap pulled low, concentrated on the five. Seth folded the paper, got up, and followed the small group at a discrete distance. Jason's and Seth's paths crossed just outside the park; they looked like strangers pursuing their own interests.

Near Broad Street, one of the kinetics suddenly collapsed and convulsed on the sidewalk. Another fell, and then two more. The kill team froze in place. Advancing further was suicide. Ambulance sirens wailed in the distance. Seth slunk into a doorway a block away, seeking a place to rest; he felt as weak as a kitten.

Jason broke off the attack as Seth's energy ran out. Rodney's training had proved indispensable. Three kinetics and a seer were down and not likely to return to the fight. Sitting on the steps and leaning against the pedestal on which stood a statue of George Washington, Jason rested, having exerted himself to the fullest. Surrounded by normal people, he could have continued the attack using their energy, but he decided he had done enough. Besides, it wasn't their fight.

Jason chuckled to himself. "No need to steal from you today."

☆   ☆   ☆

Self-interest, winning at all costs, and simple bewilderment wriggled like maggots on rotten meat in Rodney's mind. Fret and fear exhausted him. It allowed him nightly dreamless sleep but tortured his waking hours. He sat at the dinner table waiting; his survival depended on Jason's success. The induced telepathic blindness caged his savage desires to destroy the Sutter people.

Jason and Seth had not yet returned from their escapade. A healthy return of those two would set the stage for his further planning. *Seth has to be a seer*, he thought. *The kid could not generate that kind of energy on his own.* He would have to be careful around what he had thought was a normal person and his mother.

Rodney turned and looked at the winding stairway to the second floor, where his last victim of the previous war, Elizabeth Sutter, recovered. He also felt the painstakingly slow improvement to his body's strength. His fingers tapped the table in sequence; they sped up as he considered the stairs. The possible outcomes worried him: quick death, slow death, or possible negotiations to a shared, win-win goal.

The chair scraped on the floor as he pushed it back; he rose to his feet. His legs still stiff, he moved painfully slow. At the base of the iron stairs, he tapped his knuckles on the railing. He knocked on the reverberating metal again when there was no response. A pair of legs appeared at the top and came down a few steps.

"Mrs. Stiles, I believe?" He did not try to be pleasant or smile. Only hatred waited for him up those stairs.

Sarah seethed. "What do you want?"

"Tell Mrs. Sutter that I would like to talk to her about what is coming." He thought for a second. "Tell her . . . this is necessary for her son to win."

Sarah disappeared from the steps and returned a moment later. "Come up."

Getting to the second floor was harder than he expected. No helping hands aided him on the last few steps. His body demanded that he stop and take deep breaths; his head, dizzy from the effort, fell to his arm, which rested on the railing.

"Good god," he sighed.

When Rodney stood upright on the second floor, Elizabeth sat in her chair, with Sarah in waiting. He had no need of mind-reading techniques to comprehend the loathing in her eyes. This would be an audience with no chair for the supplicant. His atrophied muscles would not allow him to stay on his feet. Rodney shuffled forward and then collapsed to his knees before the women. Taking a moment to prepare and catch his breath, he slowly raised his head.

"You are aware of the action your son engages in this day?" Rodney barely got the words out. He breathed deep; his pounding heart complaining.

"I am well aware." Elizabeth's voice filled the room. "What do you want?"

"I have provided the best techniques so that your son succeeds." He sat back on his heels and raised a hand. "A minute, please? It's too hard to breathe." His weary head hung down.

He looked up when he felt Elizabeth's mental touch. Suddenly renewed, he said, "Thank you." Recognition of her improved psychic condition settled some of the old man's internal debates about which side should be his.

"Again," she said impatiently. "Get to the point. What do you want?"

"You could just take them." He smiled wanly but received no response. Accepting that he would have to speak the words, he said, "I believe we all need to work together. Samantha Black is the sideshow. It is Reena Sorenson and Community Central that we need to fear and prepare for."

Elizabeth nodded and added, "I am well aware of these things." She reached behind her and took Sarah's hand. "I know how you tracked my son to end him. I know the sacrifices"—she squeezed Sarah's hand—"made to see him safe away from you."

"Yes, yes, yes. I hate you; you hate me." Rodney, carelessly impatient, could not believe how the past never remained the past; it should, to his way thinking. *That was then; this is now. Get over it.*

"The past tells me what you will do, Rodney Davenport." *Maybe I should kill you now, and save much trouble.* Elizabeth turned away from her pathetic enemy on his knees.

"You have read my thoughts. I am helpless before you." Rodney's thought games and strategies had evaporated; he knew where his loyalties needed to stand. "You tell me what I will do for your son." Rodney feared her extraordinary strength in full bloom. She had returned, with her herculean son at her side. Awe described the little, worn-out man's reaction to the reality of his situation in Elizabeth's presence.

"Keep faith with my son and you live." Her eyes blazed. "Betray him, and I will have your sorry existence one tortured brain cell at a time until you beg for death."

Rodney shuddered. "As it should be." The small, unintended thought—freedom—lodged among his larger ones.

Elizabeth turned. "Sarah? Please make Mr. Davenport more comfortable. We have a few things to discuss." Sarah quickly produced a chair and helped Rodney into it. He expressed his gratitude.

"Now, Rodney Davenport, once again, what do you have in mind?"

☆   ☆   ☆

"Like, I don't know, man," said Russ on the phone with Jason the night before his action against the kill teams. "It's just gotten kinda weird here."

Jason sat at his desk, studying the maps of city. He glanced up to see an unconscious Rodney on his cot far across the room.

"How weird?" The unexpected call had surprised Jason. Hearing Russ's voice put him back in the toolshed with Russ on one side and Suzy on the other: a comforting image.

"Well, it's Suzy. She's not right, if you know what I mean."

"Russ, come on, man. How could I know what you mean?" Jason laughed and cringed on the inside at the same time. This was vintage Russ Wyatt.

"Yeah, I get your point." He breathed hard into the receiver. "She's talkin' to herself. She's doing all the stuff she needs to do, ya know. It's just she keeps saying stuff like 'too long' or 'he promised.'"

"Is that all, Russ?" Jason recalled his conversation with Suzy about how long he might be gone.

"No, man. If that were it, I wouldn't be on the phone." Russ's frustration filtered through the phone line. "She's not there, man. She does what she has to and nothing else. Crying all the time. Staying by herself. Sleeping a lot—more than she used to. I'm kinda worried, man. Know what I mean?"

"I don't know what I can do, Russ." Jason reached out his right hand; he cradled the phone base and pulled it closer in a caress. "I can try to get down there after classes and tests and stuff. Do you think she can hold out until then? Like December, maybe?"

"I guess." Russ sighed. "I'll do what I can. Your foster dad has been trying to help too. He's a pretty good guy."

"Yeah, he is." Jason thought a moment. "Ya know, I never sent you my new phone number. How'd you get it?"

"Your doctor, man. He passed it around."

"Oh, okay." Jason realized Dr. Lipton had received his letter. He changed the subject. "What's happening with Patti? She still okay?"

"Yeah, she's fine. I have to say, though . . .

Jason hung up twenty minutes later, overjoyed to hear from his best friend but worried about Suzy and the fact that Lipton had shared his phone number. What was happening in Franklin Chase?

Chapter 17

Hiram Lipton made the calls, set up the logistics, and called the meeting, which met at the Wyatt's house in Franklin Chase. In front of the living-room fireplace, he checked his list against the people in the room. A slight tremor in his hands signaled the doctor's stress at addressing this group of strangers. Most shared last year's August event under the sanctuary oak tree with Jason, where they sat in a semicircle before him: Mr. and Mrs. Downing, Louise Deloro, Professor Chiang Chen, Russ Wyatt, and Suzy. The second tier included Mr. and Mrs. Wyatt, their hosts, who sat behind the love seat in support of their son, Russ, and his friend Suzy. Frank, Suzy's chauffeur for the evening and foster father, leaned on the mahogany record player where Jason had learned about Sinatra, the King, and the Beatles.

Lipton put away his list and patted his sport coat's pockets as he spoke, "You all have received a copy of Jason's letter." He found his pipe and the spindle of pipe accessories. "Some of you know what I know." He ignored the semicircle of eyes fixed on him, scraped the pipe's bowl, and then continued. "For your own protection, some of you are no longer aware." Lipton reached into the fireplace and tapped the upside-down pipe against the scorched brick. "A few here suspect, but do not believe in their suspicions."

"Do you mind if I smoke, Mrs. Wyatt?" Lipton held up his pipe with a hopeful smile.

"Of course not, doctor." Peg Wyatt clung to her husband's hand. Harry Wyatt looked confused, not sure why they were there.

"Tonight I will clarify the points in the letter I received from Jason. If possible, we will have the truth of it." He tapped down the pipe tobacco and produced a lighter. The pulled flame filled the pipe bowl, and soon blue smoke rose toward the ceiling. He looked around the room at the rapt audience. He removed the pipe with his left hand and began.

"Jason Sutter came to me for treatment not too long after he was in the Dubois house." Lipton pointed with the pipe at Frank in the back of the room. Jason's foster father nodded. "His chart indicated he was psychotic and heard voices." Lipton considered his audience for a moment. "I now know, on one level, the report was accurate. On another, it was completely wrong. The voices, you see, were real or, more to the point, real people's thoughts. Jason"—he paused for emphasis—"is a telepath."

At this news, there was a simultaneous intake of breath from all but Russ and Suzy.

"For reasons we do not need to go into tonight, Jason was free of medication for most of his time with me." Lipton shook his head. "Without the drugs, his behavior was within normal limits. So he was not nuts, as the kids might say." He stopped to allow that fact to sink in.

"Why are we here, doctor?" asked the well-turned-out Louise Deloro in a tasteful forest-green business dress with matching accessories. She aimed her mischievous smile at Lipton.

"My dear lady, you, your sister, Kyle, and Professor Chen knew this in August of last year. You helped our Jason by allowing his abilities to feed on your energy to make everyone forget about the tabloid article."

"Which article was that?" she asked. She could not imagine that she or her sister would take any tabloid article seriously.

"This one." Lipton handed out two copies showing Jason and Sally Tilghman on the front page with the main article, "Cure at Kearny State." The copies made their way around the room.

"Oh god. I remember something about this." Mary's hand covered her mouth; she turned to her sister, who nodded.

"Doctor?" Chiang raised his hand.

"Yes, Professor Chen."

"I also recall flowers growing in my landlady's garden that should not be able to do so. I believe this had something to do with Jason." Chiang stared at the floor and rubbed his temples to release memories.

"I would ask you to stop trying to pry open your recollections. There are greater issues at stake at this point." Lipton pulled on his pipe and blew a stream of smoke to the ceiling. He waited.

The room quieted. They focused on him.

"Jason," said the good doctor, his pipe transferred to his right hand, "came to us wounded. There were whole communities of persons with his abilities. A civil war, however, raged among them. Jason's wounding saved his life. Needless to say, the wrong side won. His family was destroyed and unknown to him." He stopped. His left hand wiped a film of sweat from his forehead. The story was just too big; there was so much to say.

Lipton extended his hands and said, "Suzy and Russ know all of this too well. Jason confided in them from the earliest time at school in Franklin Chase. Then, of course, Jason saved Russ's sister, Patti, from the deadly attack."

"What?" Mrs. Wyatt was on her feet, advancing with Mr. Wyatt at her side.

"Stop, Mom, Dad!" yelled Russ. He spun and knelt against the love seat back. "She's okay. It's all okay because of Jason." His outburst froze his parents. He looked from one to the other and said, "Believe me, I know. It's okay."

Lipton watched as Peg and Harry stared at their son. They found it hard to calm. Harry looked to Lipton to say something, then back to Russ, constantly moving his hands. Then the couple returned to their seats, simultaneously deciding to trust their son.

"I would now like to bring up two persons who share Jason's specialness." Lipton pulled Russ and Suzy from the love seat and kept them on either side of him. "They can answer a good many of your questions better than I."

The tsunami of questions went on for a long time. Suzy and Russ told them everything they knew. They left nothing out as they explained to Frank where Lydia's headaches had come from. Dumbfounded, he sat and nodded every now and then. Peg and Harry Wyatt did not know how to deal with the news of their youngest daughter's hidden abilities along with Russ's proven talents. They wondered what that meant they were.

"Jason always tried to do good," Suzy said.

"Well now, Lipton," said Downing, "you have provided a vivid cock-and-bull story that I absolutely believe to be true. This lines up with, shall we say, things in my life and past that have found resolution with Mr. Sutter's presence." He put his arm around Mary. "This, however, is all in the past. What does the boy need right now?"

"He needs me." Lipton smiled. "He desperately needs his power sources. And more to the point, he needs the people whom he knows care about him. He needs you."

"Well, we all can't just pick up and leave for New York." Mary's thoughtful frown was mirrored on other faces.

"That, dear people, is why we are here," said Lipton. "How do we do for him what he has done for us? How do we do him some good?"

The gathering went on beyond midnight as stubborn details found resolution. Finally the meeting broke up with plans that needed only practical consideration for execution. Russ trudged up the stairs to his bedroom, while Suzy and Frank headed out the front door.

"Russ and Suzy!" called Lipton. "Do not tell Jason." They turned to him and nodded.

Russ captured the gist of their thoughts: "He'd only get all superhero and tell us to stay out of it for our own good."

☆   ☆   ☆

Failure induced anger, and fear made a bitter brew; stress tied Samantha Black's guts into Gordian knots. It had been two days since the failed attack. She had stopped eating due to the pain; no position brought comfort. Sleep darted away from her every time her exhausted body drew near it. Collapsed in her desk chair, she stared at the phone. Hours passed.

That phone on her desk in the Tarrytown house, once inanimate and quiet, started taunting her. "Call Reena. Get it over with. She's not totally unreasonable, sort of." Samantha picked up the receiver and dialed. "Good girl," cooed the phone. "My cord is strong." Before her "huh?" escaped her lips, she sank through the floor; a drowning quicksand trapped her. The curled wire stretched, and she slipped further. Her hands clung to the receiver as she sank deeper.

The phone rang, blasting away the terror of Samantha's short dream. Her head shot off the desk; the swivel chair caught her as she flung herself back. She stared at the clamoring torture device.

"I am sorry, Rodney," she whispered, sure she was the next in line for total reduction, for extraction. She lifted the dead weight of judgment from its cradle.

"Hello."

"Report," insisted Reena.

"We sent out two teams." The robot Samantha took over; human reactions were wasted breath. "One started at the southern tip of the island the other at Thirty-Fourth Street on the east side, heading south. We searched in acceptable patterns, intending to link up at the Flat Iron Building."

"Results."

"Three kinetics and one seer are out of action. Nothing found. No contact made." Samantha believed her boss already knew these facts. Certainty of execution left a person resigned and quiet, or fiery and defiant. Samantha kept her mouth shut.

"Your strategy made sense, given what we knew then." Reena paused. "We know more now. You were set up, Samantha. Your enemy was likely right in front of you."

Samantha leaned on the desk, held the receiver tighter to her ear, and massaged her temple with her other hand. "I'm sorry. I don't understand. What are you saying?"

"There are powers present in your area for which you are not prepared. Your losses were much less than they could have been. You did well under the circumstances."

A dull, gray dawn of hope grew in Samantha's eastern sky. Questions exploded in her mind. But her body relaxed; her guts uncoiled. She would survive.

"Ask them," commanded Reena a thousand miles away.

"Who?"

"Elizabeth Sutter and her fourteen-year-old son, plus two seers. We were unaware of the seers previously."

"You can see them?" *A simple question*, thought Samantha, still amazed that she would get through this episode unscathed. The pressure on her ear decreased; her hand lay on the desk, fingers spread.

"No, I can't, which is why you were unable to track them."

"In that case, and I mean no disrespect, how do you know this and what must I do for us to win?" Samantha absentmindedly swept her hand across the smooth desktop and then sat back. Relief fell like a soaking rain on draught-stricken earth, penetrating head to toe; she was not responsible.

"Rodney Davenport wants reinstatement." Samantha sat up straight and clutched the desk's edge. "He, of all people," Reena said with a chuckle, "called me with a proposal."

"Proposal?" This did not sound good from Samantha's point of view.

"I am inclined to go with it. He provided all the latest information and why you suffered the losses you did. What he did to you"—she paused for emphasis—"he is willing to do to them for the right price."

"And . . ." Samantha said.

"And Rodney is ever the conniving, little worm he has always been. He has his talents, I must admit." Samantha could picture Reena coiling her hair around her finger as she gave Davenport credit for the dirty work.

"But you can't confirm his position. You are going with his history." Samantha sat rock-solid still. Her implied assertion that Reena might not have total control could hurt her.

"It is a reasonable assertion based on prior experience. I will know for sure if your next report never comes. Won't I?"

Samantha swallowed. The hook she dangled on was sharp and held her fast. There was no escape from the next battle, which would set the pieces on the chessboard in new positions.

"I request," Samantha asked politely, "that you give me what you have, and a new battle plan will be created here."

"Good. We understand one another?"

"Completely."

"Rodney has betrayed his saviors."

The conversation went on for another hour, covering the details of how to rebuild and prepare.

✷   ✷   ✷

Jason checked his watch. "Oh jeez! I'm supposed to be in the chem lab in fifteen minutes." He and Seth had just left Washington on his pedestal and headed uptown.

"You're kidding, right?" Seth yawned and stretched, his strength only partially recovered, and then stopped to confront Jason. "You just disabled three kinetics and a seer and managed to confuse two telepaths. How can you want to go to some . . . some class?" Seth looked at him as if he were nuts.

True to his word that something would be worked out, Seth took the time to endure the long lines of NYU's registration process. The day of the battle, as Jason hauled down the elevator gate, Seth had handed the boy his college class schedule and said, "The ID looks like me. So lose this one and get a new one."

With the street battle over feeling exhausted, Seth yelled, "Are you totally insane?!"

"I don't know. I just want to go." Jason put his arm on Seth's shoulder. "I can't explain it. There is just too much to learn. I hav'ta get started. "He stood. "You want to come along?"

"Hell no!"

Jason could tell that Seth considered his decision to be suicidal. But the big guy relented, saying, "I'll come along anyway." He started walking uptown, and Jason heard him mumble, "Some dumb-ass class that doesn't mean anything. Get us both killed."

Seth stood guard, leaning against the wall outside the double-door entrance to the lab. Jason stood in line, looking around. The freshmen chemistry lab needed work on its infrastructure. The small sinks at the end of each of four long islands had rusting faucets that dripped steadily.

The lab's paint-peeled walls and ceiling, plus the old-style fans that turned and launched dust filaments that floated gently to the stone-topped tables, heralded where freshmen stood in the university hierarchy: dirt bottom.

"Needs paint," said Jason, laughing to himself.

"Ha!" came from the guy directly behind him in line. Jason swung around and faced a freshman with a devil-may-care grin. He liked him immediately. The young man had dark, curly hair and brown eyes that promised limit pushing to the point of trouble; he was an older version of Russ.

"What can I say?" He spoke unabashedly and stuck out his hand. "Roy. Premed."

"Jason. Not sure yet." He smiled and shook the taller eighteen-year-old's hand.

"Boy wonder?" asked Roy.

"That's what they tell me," Jason said with a sigh.

While the thirty freshmen stood in line, the lab rules and regulations were spelled out by a professor's assistant: no poisoning yourself or burning down the lab.

Roy laughed quietly. "I'll have to check on who mixed what together to start a fire." He scanned the room and decided which table to try to get. "You're definitely in my study group . . . if you wanna be."

"Sure." Jason was flattered that someone older had included him. He wondered about the student or students who poisoned themselves.

"No doubt," said Roy, "I will need talent on my side to pass this course."

"Besides," whispered Jason leaning toward Roy, "the girls will feel more comfortable around a kid."

"Man!" Roy stared at Jason, winked, and then slapped him on the back. "It's like you were reading my mind."

Chapter 18

Jason and Seth returned from their mission and the must-attend, two-hour chemistry lab to a very unpleasant scene. As the elevator gates rose, Jason heard his mom's laughter. He and Seth turned the corner to find the enemies trading stories in his apartment at his dinner table.

Elizabeth laughed out loud at her son's apparent disapproval of her being with Rodney. Their easy, animated conversation upset Jason very much.

"We," said Elizabeth, catching her breath, "were talking about life before the troubles started. It wasn't all bad."

Jason leveled his most displeased expression at her. He saw her eyes glitter, holding back tears of laughter at the absurdity of the scene.

"This particular old guy," Jason said, emphasizing every word, "almost murdered my friend's sister and did not hesitate to bring you and your husband down." Jason stood before them with arms folded; the wrongness of the scene wreaked havoc on his expectation of his mother's propriety. It was not seemly to be so engaged with this man. It struck him as a betrayal of her husband, his father.

"Young man, what do you think we are doing here?" asked Rodney, annoyed. "Are you completely insane? Stupid social convention has no place in a time of war!" The old man rose and pointed at Jason. "Now pull up a seat and tell us what happened. This is critically important, and we have been waiting a long time." Jason rolled his eyes and looked at Elizabeth.

"Trust me?" Her gentle smile and simple question tore Jason from his adolescent, high-ground argument for right and wrong encounters.

"Sorry." He nodded, embarrassed, and took a place at the table.

"It went precisely as you said it would." Jason held Rodney's eyes with a glare; a level of defiance for his father's sake remained. "Three kinetics are down." Then he said louder, over his shoulder, "Seth thinks that several telepaths and seers took hits also."

"I do," responded Seth, who had abandoned Jason for the kitchen confines; dinner preparations were underway. The large copper skillet banged on a burner on the gas range.

"Remarkable," whispered Rodney.

"It is something . . . unexpected," said Elizabeth. "It changes things."

"What?" asked Jason.

"Seth is not a seer," stated Rodney. "Yet you could use him as a source to maintain and support your attack." A slow nod of his head punctuated Rodney's answer.

How much does he know? The unspoken question went to his mother.

She smiled, and her message entered his mind gently. *Enough to help, not hurt. For the moment, he is aligned with us.*

"Young man, I am not a fool." Rodney leaned toward Jason. "Your mother has many, many reasons to detest the ground upon which I walk." He nodded toward Elizabeth. With a defiant, arrogant sneer, he continued. "You can destroy me whenever you wish. I know this. Your mother knows that she needs a vicious attack dog to help you beat the odds. You, young man, need a killer's training."

Equally as angry, Jason exerted pressure. "I am no killer and I don't want to be."

"Stop," commanded Rodney as the pain blurred his vision. "Are you going to become me?"

Jason stopped instantly. "Never!" The very thought twisted his stomach. "I guess I should say sorry . . . but I won't." He slouched in his chair, arms folded.

"At his age," whispered Rodney, "that's remarkable control. I would have murdered the insolent interloper if pushed like this."

Elizabeth's hand grasped Rodney's arm. "Are you satisfied?"

"Yes, lady." Rodney bowed his head and climbed out of his chair as best he could. He looked back at Jason. "I have a phone call to make." He rose from the table and shambled to Jason's desk at the other end of the apartment.

Elizabeth just smiled at her son, adding no new information as Rodney made his slow, stiff-jointed way to a phone. Jason stared at her, chagrined. He could steal what he wanted to know from the defenseless Rodney, but it would be wrong. Nevertheless, something was going on between those two; some strategy had been set, and he knew nothing of it.

"You used to laugh a lot more." Seth studied the linguini on his fork. A drop of garlic-laced oil and wine fell back to the chicken marsala on his plate. Jason looked up; his knife and fork hovered in midcut.

"There's nothing to joke about." Jason still chafed over the encounter before dinner with his mother and Davenport.

"You misunderstand," Seth said. "I meant when you were younger, when it was just you and me doing stuff together . . . before the war." Seth, the de facto maitre d' for the current Sutter household, cooked, cleaned up, and collected red wines. He raised his wine glass and sipped one of his choicest Chianti vintages.

"Was it a war or an insurgency? Those others never call it a war." Chicken with a piece of mushroom finally found its way to Jason's mouth.

"War . . . insurgency." Seth shrugged. "More of you died than all the normal people in the world wars, as a percentage of the population." The wine glass warmed in the huge hand as he watched Jason eat. "So why don't you?"

"What?" Jason picked up his glass of lemonade; his eyes held Seth's peering down the length of the glass.

"Laugh very much."

"It's not your fault." Jason put down his sweating tumbler and turned it in place, studying the water marks trailing the twists. "My mother, father, you and your mother, and, I guess, me from back then—all gone."

Seth nodded.

Jason continued. "I had to do that to a friend's little sister."

Seth looked up from twirling pasta on his fork, surprised.

"Not a complete wipe like my mother did to me . . . just enough to protect her from him." Jason glanced at upward, where his mother, Sarah, and Rodney Davenport strategized over Seth's wonderfully cooked meal.

"Ah." Seth put down his fork and wiped his mouth with the napkin from his lap. "That would explain your bad mood."

"Well, they're up to something and won't tell me." He pushed his plate forward and then sat forward and leaned on his elbows. "I mean, this is life and death, after all. Ya know?"

"And you're not sure your mother understands this?" Seth poured more wine into his glass.

"No." Jason shook his head. "That's not it."

"Then you are attempting to be your missing father and defend the family?" The big hand lifted the glass in a toast to the gallant son. "Is that it?"

"You're being difficult. Do you know that?" Jason felt childish. His embarrassed grin signaled that Seth had cut to the heart of the matter. "It just isn't right . . . or something. Oh, I don't know. I just don't like it, okay?"

The big man nodded and said, "So what will you do?"

"Trust her. What else?" Jason raised his tumbler. Seth took stem in hand and touched his glass to it. The glasses rang as they toasted the obvious.

✫   ✫   ✫

The Badlands Hotel near Bismarck, North Dakota, expected to start their slow business stretch from late autumn to early spring. But it went the other way. Some Community something or other occupied an entire wing and owned their largest conference room for a week, possibly longer. Caught shorthanded, the Badlands owner doubled the wages of any summer college help that would stay the extra week. The full-time long-timers received extra paid vacation for working the strange convention; they usually took off while the weather remained tame.

The delay to their plans increased as the very quiet convention with excessively polite conventioneers stretched to two weeks. The money was good; no one complained. None of the employees recalled any discussions from the many times they floated in and out of the hall, refilling coffee urns, replacing water pitchers, and delivering food.

Reena dressed comfortably in pants that Samantha would approve: loose fitting, khaki, multipocket. Her black, short-sleeved top projected femininity: form fitting, revealing. With her hair pulled back, her eyes and high cheekbones were accentuated. These were intentional distractions.

She held center stage at the open end of tables in a horseshoe arrangement. The Community heads and their lieutenants waited patiently for her opening remarks. They had come from the South, Southwest, West, Midwest, and Northwest organizations; three or four foot soldiers per each attending member maintained security outside the hotel. In the room, it was an even mix of male to female in power positions. They were a very sober group—war hardened and not easily convinced to take the field again.

Reena studied the eyes and saw the concern around the tables. She said, "In the next few days, we may be at war once again." She allowed the buzz in the room to settle before she continued. "You will note that neither Rodney nor his replacement, Samantha, are with us. Rodney may be dead, a double agent for us, or a traitor. We will have to wait and see. Samantha and her crew may or may not be prepared for what they will confront. This we will know shortly."

Reena stepped to the right and slowly walked the table's curve while she spoke. "The enemy has taken ground and held it." She sensed a question and turned to face the questioner. "Yes," she replied, "part of the Sutter clan has risen. It seems we will have to fight an old battle." She continued her slow pass back to the front of the room. "While we are together, we have to muster our forces, organize our resources, and prepare for an all-out assault in New York.

"And we may face something new. Samantha's efforts will tell the tale." No telepathy was needed to sense the dis-ease in the room. "I will take questions."

The Southwest leader removed his black Stetson from his full head of salt-and-pepper hair and tossed it down on the table. "The sacrificial lamb is the Northeast Community?" he asked. He sat back with a stern look on his rugged features and waited for confirmation of the question in everyone's mind. "How exactly do we get the information we need if Samantha's people are all dead?"

"Yes to your first question." Reena smiled pleasantly. "As to your second point, I have dispatched observers who will be out of harm's way." Heads nodded. This made sense.

"What's the problem?" asked a slender woman in jeans and a white peasant blouse with a Southern lilt—the Southern Community leader.

"I can't . . ." Reena folded her arms and looked to the back of the room. She suddenly missed Bill, who she had left behind at home. "I can't see the enemy." A heavy quiet burdened the room.

"Am I correct, honey, in guessing that this is a temporary setback?" The leaders leaned forward in anticipation of her answer. Who among them would take her place if a weakness developed in her abilities?

"I don't know." Lying or hedging the truth was not a good idea. She could not afford to show any weakness with these people. If she was to start a war, she would be out front leading it. Her power remained the greatest wielded by one person. She knew it, but did they need reminding? "Ask me in a few days."

"So," began the West leader, tall, tan, and wearing a Hawaiian shirt, "if Samantha is unsuccessful, then we"—he waved his hands to indicate the tables—"converge on New York City for an all-out search and destroy?"

"Yes. I will take the lead with all my people ready to go."

The leaders around the table captured the reactions of their fellows and projected their unhappiness. Sorenson was not handling the situation to their satisfaction. If this opposition became well organized and grew, it could lead to another all-out war.

"It's settled," declared Reena, ignoring the worry in her audience. "As soon as I know, you will be informed. Form your teams. Get organized for a big push when needed. We do not want to return to chaos with normans everywhere, ready to destroy us. We will meet and conquer this challenge!"

Her final comment fell flat. The other leaders remained silent, unimpressed, and unsure. They rose together and filed out of the room.

✫   ✫   ✫

Two cars, a black Mercedes and a blue Pontiac Le Mans, rushed north on the turnpike from Franklin Chase. Harry Wyatt drove the Le Mans. Chiang Chen rode shotgun. Russ and Suzy shared the back seat. Lipton carried the Downings and Louise in the Mercedes.

After the first thirty minutes, the conversation died in both vehicles. The only sounds were the wind rushing over the windows and the sixty-five-mile-an-hour whine of tires on blacktop. Lipton's therapeutic failures haunted his thoughts. If only he had a Jason to support his efforts, he could help even the most difficult patients. His talk with Jason at dinner one night before returning to Pennsylvania replayed over and over, torturing and amazing him.

"Some days," Jason had said, "I was punch-drunk from the medication. Lydia and Frank still had me join the other children at a meal. Of course, I wasn't all that sure if anything was real." Jason told the doctor about being fed: when a fork with food hovered at this mouth, he ate.

"I never said much, just watched. Kinda out of it, ya know." Jason paused. "Once, I was mesmerized by one kid's lips moving, but the words did not match what I heard." Jason had stopped eating and looked around the restaurant.

"That kid might have said, 'That guy plays like a girl,' but I heard clearly, 'I'm nothing. I'll never be good enough.' I laughed out loud. It was like a really bad dubbing in one of those monster movies. The other kids laughed at my outburst. Called me a nut job. But . . ." Jason leaned forward. "I saw a shadowy adult woman behind the boy; she bent down and whispered in his ear. The kid laughed about something. The shadow woman smiled derisively and became transparent."

"I recall another kid had this dark, cloud-like thing hovering behind and around him. It sent black tendrils floating in and out of his nose, mouth, and ears like smoke. It was just too weird. I heard when he was not speaking, 'It's my fault Tommy died. It's my fault. Mommy said so.'"

Lipton had stared at Jason, aghast. Before him sat a tool able to identify the source of neurosis; he was a psychotherapist's dream. Jason then went on to describe the many specters hovering about the other children at that long-ago dinner table.

Flying up the New Jersey Turnpike, Lipton occupied his mind contemplating the possible physical brain corrections with Jason by his side, including cures for manic depressive disorder and schizophrenia.

"What am I doing?" whispered Lipton. Distracted by his healing daydream, the speedometer had pushed toward seventy miles per hour. He released the accelerator slightly; the car to his right signaled, and he allowed it to pull in front. "Pay attention to the road," Lipton uttered louder. An honest conversation with Jason and, the doctor assumed, his mother, would decide if his dream made sense.

"What was that, doctor?" asked Downing, who had dozed off with his head against the headrest.

"You were going to tell me more stories about your experiences with Jason, Mr. Downing." Lipton signaled and moved to the right lane. The car settled to just over the speed limit. "There was a ping-pong game at your first meeting?"

"Ha!" Downing slapped his leg. "Jason was a trooper. I remember lunch, my doctor's worried face, and not much else . . . I felt better; I know that." Downing stared out the window. "A rollercoaster comes to mind."

Lipton took a split second to look at Downing and then riveted his eyes back to the road.

"Don't bother asking." Downing shrugged. "With any luck we will know in about fifty miles."

The green and white sign posting the distance to the city limits came and went.

Chapter 19

"How do you know?" asked Jason when he and Rodney went over the plan for the tenth time. They studied the building layout, an unfinished skyscraper, spread out on Jason's dinner table. Seth puttered about in the kitchen, humming to himself.

"I left you without an escape route." The old guy chortled at his cleverness. "The stairs and the external elevator are the only ways in or out. They will cover both and approach from both."

"I don't get why they will fall for this. I wouldn't." Jason stood up, still examining the map. Rodney turned and looked up at the boy.

"Haven't you been paying any attention?" Rodney sighed heavily. "Okay, okay." He calmed. "One more time . . . they're ignorant. They did not do their homework. Arrogance and a surety of their invincibility blind them. And . . ." Rodney slapped the building drawing and grinned. "They do not know about you."

Jason had heard this before and was not sure he bought the entire "you're different" argument. He grasped the plan but playing the hinge pin on which their strategy turned meant those differences had better exist; he had his doubts.

"Just follow the plan!" Rodney pointed at the building drawing. "Disable their kinetics; then match energy with energy until they exhaust their sources. I leave it to you and your mother to deal with what happens next. I would just end them all, right then and there." He stood. His physical recovery left him able to get around unstooped and free of a shuffle. "You two have other ideas. Stupid, but . . ." He shrugged.

When the plan was fully memorized, the sky was darkening with the waning sun. The elevator gates at Jason's apartment parted, and a crowd of people piled onto the open floor. He choked, and iced tea shot out through his nose. He jumped up. The chair spilled backward and clattered on the floor; the table scraped an inch out of alignment.

"Chiang?" Jason stared in disbelief. He quickly grabbed a napkin and wiped his face.

Russ pushed to the front. "Jason . . . man! Ya gonna invite us in or what?"

Jason hugged his friend, and the others followed Russ. Hands were shaken and hugs given. Jason felt Suzy standing back by the elevator gate. As he turned, when their eyes met, the world's occupants collapsed to two. Normal humans at their ages would never experience such a connection. No touching could ever be as intimate. Their thoughts and feelings wove in and around their minds like sea otters at play in a warm, inviting tidal pool.

Jason left the group, and Lipton pulled Seth over to the group for introductions. Dazed, Jason calmly walked to Suzy, who took his hand and squeezed.

"I missed you." She smiled.

"Russ called me. He was a little concerned." Jason could not take his eyes from hers. The act of speaking was a distraction. After a few silent minutes, everything that needed knowing between them was known. They broke off their inner excavations temporarily to join the others.

Jason addressed his guests. "I am so glad to see you all and scared to death that this may be a terrible mistake." He took a moment to capture each face. He saw all their smiles and hopes. Fear for their survival wrapped about him like cellophane, paralyzing him and choking off his voice.

"What'd I tell ya?" Russ said as he accepted a tall drink from Seth. "He's getting all superhero."

He ignored Russ's comment and said, "Dr. Lipton, does my mother know?"

"I do believe she does. It was, however, a Mr. Davenport who acted as our agent in this endeavor." Lipton began to search his pockets for his hide-and-seek playing pipe.

"Jason," said Chiang. He put his hand on the doctor's shoulder, which stopped Lipton's patting down of his jacket. "I would like to meet your mother. I believe we have much to discuss and little time left."

Elizabeth welcomed the strangers but could not totally accept that normal people could be so devoted to her son like Sarah and Seth were to her and her family. It had taken years to build those relationships. With Rodney seated nearby and Sarah at her shoulder, she set aside her concern and accepted them. They were there on her son's behalf. Rodney and Sarah were introduced. She sent an unspoken request to Jason.

Instantly Jason's friends' blocked memories found freedom and informed their owners. All heads swiveled to Jason; they were stunned by their experience of Jason's thoughts in their heads.

When Chiang recovered from his initial shock, he asked a simple question: "What do you need us to do?"

Downing, Mary, Louise, and Russ's dad, Harry, came up behind Chiang and waited patiently for their marching orders. No questions, no recriminations, and no hesitation.

✧   ✧   ✧

The skyscraper's incomplete superstructure pushed up through the soil, towering over the surrounding brownstone buildings. Jason sat on an overturned rivet bucket on the twenty-first floor. The smooth concrete floor stretched in all directions, ending at open-air ledges dropping hundreds of feet to the stacks of lumber, piles of pipes, construction trailers, and concrete mixers below. Heavy steel-beam columns supporting the layers above pushed through the glazed surface. The full moon's light reflected off the surface, and dim rainbows spread from the beam's edges.

The cold metal rivets rested in a neat pile a few feet to the right of Jason's bucket throne. The cool October air whipped through his exposed position. Acetylene tanks on chained hand trucks rested against several columns. Hand and power tools lay piled together near the temporary, caged elevator for transporting workers. With his hands clasped over his knees, Jason waited.

Tonight they would learn where Rodney Davenport's loyalties truly belonged. Either Jason, his mother, and all their supporters would be dead or the Northeast Community would be forever changed. Rodney would survive either way. They had left him on his own at the apartment, safe from retaliation from either side.

Five stories below, where the finished outer walls kept the wind out, a circle of trusted friends meditated amid stacks of plumbing pipes and huge coils of thick, electric wire. Abundant psychic energy ready for Jason's use emanated from below.

Elizabeth sat in the stairwell halfway to the twenty-second level. She was wrapped in a blanket and perched on the folding stepladder used in Seth's kitchen. Harry sat on the first step below her.

Two days earlier, in a quiet conversation with his father, Russ had said, "There's a pretty good chance that you're gonna be asked to do stuff you never knew you could." Harry stared at him, confused. Before the roles and responsibilities circulated to the team, Harry had approached Elizabeth. He interrupted Jason who spoke quietly with his mother.

"Russ seems to think I might be some kind of low-level seer, as you people call them." Elizabeth noted his discomfort as his hands played with the car keys and change in his pockets and he rocked back and forth. "Maybe . . . um . . . maybe I could do something?"

Elizabeth smiled, charmed by the offer. Jason looked at Harry critically.

Then Jason grinned. "Try him; Russ has rarely been wrong." He turned to Mr. Wyatt. "Don't tell him I said that. I'll never hear the end of it."

"Yes," Elizabeth said after a short pause. "He will do very nicely." She grabbed Peg's information from Harry's mind and found her in Franklin Chase, taking care of their daughters. Patti was very interesting; she almost glowed with power. Jason's shield over her had begun to wear thin in places, but the energy provided by Harry enabled Elizabeth to reach over the distances without exhaustion.

In the stairwell, Harry sneezed. A fine, fresh concrete dust filled the stairwell air. "Excuse me." He wiped his nose.

"God bless you, Harry," said Elizabeth.

"Thanks," he replied. "You know I am not at all sure about this."

"Mr. Wyatt," Elizabeth said calmly, "you are a very adequate seer, which is especially needed this night. When this is all over, we will talk about what it all means."

Harry nodded.

Elizabeth was glad for his company. The plan called for her to project her power, if needed. Otherwise she would handle the aftermath: the vanquished required careful consideration. She knew that plans and the reality of the battlefield did not always align. She prepared herself.

Jason sat on his short, rusted throne alone until three shadows came onto the field. The psychic pressure came instantly; he easily balanced the attack. The telepath's silent entry revealed that kinetics had raised them the many stories as scouts. They jumped onto the concrete between the beams as if they jumped from a floating platform. Jason wondered how many kinetics it would take to launch the scouts twenty-one floors.

The crank and clack of the elevator signaled more warriors could be expected shortly. He wasted no energy discovering whom he faced. It did not matter. A flood of bodies poured from the elevator: telepaths, kinetics, and normal people.

"Please, I'll give you anything you want. Don't hurt me," whined a male voice. Other voices cried out. They were normal people being dragged physically over the cement surface and then pulled to their feet. Hostages, they would be sacrificed or used as human shields if the Sutter team had their own kinetics.

"We will kill them," Samantha said as she advanced toward the sitting figure. "Surrender, and they walk away safe and sound." Among the networked minds, she posed the question. *Can any of you see this person?*

No.

Jason captured the exchange. Rodney had it right. Apparently they never considered that he would pick up their signals.

Breathless warriors entered the killing ground from the stairwell: more kinetics and telepaths. A quick count indicated that Jason's small team confronted fifteen with telekinetic ability, ten telepaths, and ten seers; it would have been an overwhelming force in typical situations experienced in the last war.

Jason met all psychic force, all attacks, with equal and opposite force, holding everything even. When a normal female hostage contorted and screamed and then floated through the air toward him, the plan took a hard right turn and crashed headlong into the unexpected.

Samantha Black laughed as the screaming woman levitated a step ahead of where she stood. Whimpers and grunts issued from the other normals as their tormentors chuckled, goading them. This was the strategy that had worked well in the previous war. In trying to save innocent people, the good guys were overwhelmed. Too much energy went into defense, with little left for offense.

"Well? How long will she have to suffer?" Samantha readied for the attack to break the energy causing the suffering. It did not come.

Jason stood up. The pile of rivets lifted off the floor and spread in an arc before him; each was marked for a kinetic. As the quiet settled in, like rockets the rivets shot to their intended targets. The targets, the kinetics, felt safe behind the hostage shield. The rivets, however, passed through the human shields as if they were ghosts, doing no apparent damage; the kinetics went down.

"How?" escaped Samantha's lips.

"You saw what you wanted to see." Jason spoke with deliberation. "I moved the normals to safety a few minutes after you arrived."

The screaming woman faded. The normal people lugged to the twenty-first floor at great expense to the seers lay unconscious to one side. Without kinetics, the normals lost a significant part of their usefulness.

"I can't use them anymore, Samantha." One of her lieutenants pointed to the normals.

"Then you can drag them over here and bludgeon them with a hammer, if I order it," she hissed. The overwhelming force strategy had failed. She had no backup plan and could not reconsider her strategic position, which was much weaker without the telekinetic warriors. Attack only drove her decisions. *Take out their kinetics*, she ordered.

"*What kinetics?*" asked several seers and telepaths.

Find and kill whoever shot the rivets, she demanded. Her team looked at each other and shrugged. Logic pointed to the only answer.

It's the boy. They all fired back in response to their leader's order.

While the meditating circle generated Jason's rocket fuel, Dr. Lipton's job was to observe and help those in the circle. If they collapsed from exhaustion or needed some medical care, he was ready. Lipton walked around the outside and logged his observations on each participant. In midsentence, he put away his pen and laid aside his log. Certain that Elizabeth was in danger, he abandoned his post and headed up the stairs. As he passed a tool belt, he pulled a utility knife from a leather pocket.

A part of his mind spun around, looking for the reason he needed to get upstairs. The invader in his mind, much stronger, controlled his every move. Lipton knew he was outmatched. He heard two voices discuss what would happen, as if he were a six-year-old in the principal's office listening to the adults talk about his need for discipline.

I've got him, said a male voice.

He's grabbed the knife. The female voice confirmed. *Where to now?*

She's somewhere above. He helped carry her up. Working together, the two voices did not give Lipton any choice. He rattled the bars of his psychic cage furiously, resisting every step.

Calm down there, buckaroo, and maybe we will leave you with a small part of your mind. Both voices chuckled. Lipton doubled his agitation. He had a rough idea of what was happening and rebelled against the obvious intent.

He's fighting, said the female.

Pain. The male voice commanded. Lipton stopped. His body did not react. The small part of his mind that was his own screamed as a thousand hammers slammed him. *You want to quiet down?* Lipton retreated in his mind to get away from the assault.

Good boy! The male took over Lipton's body. He climbed to the target, the razor sharp blade fully extended in his right hand.

Lipton's conscious mind fell back and considered his next steps. It had surprised him when they took away his free will. Yet he had discovered some things at his mind's takeover. First, Jason had kept his word not to enter his mind without permission. Lipton was wide open for attack. Second, the two controlling him were afraid.

Think, damn it. You're trained to adjust. Find out the truth. His weak voice did not receive any response from his captors. What did he know? He concentrated, careful not to expose himself to the minds controlling him. His attackers feared the unknown. Jason presented a mystery, a challenge. A lack of confidence in leadership opened them to Lipton's suggestions.

Before he reached the twenty-second story, where Elizabeth held her ground, Lipton knew the two controlling him had to be distracted. If he got lucky, they would be weaker when his hand held the knife to Elizabeth's throat.

Hey! Hey, up there! Lipton needed to plant doubt.

Quiet! The female ordered his silence. He had their attention.

What would you do to the team who killed your mother?

I said quiet! Pain hit Lipton again. His body took the steps a little slower. If he had a body under his control, Lipton would be on his knees. It was like his hand, just beginning to blacken above a flame, had been turned over to cook on the other side. He retreated.

Just thought you should know. He had the strength for one thought. *You have already lost. He is more than you know.* He could do no more; he ran from the torture and hid.

The telepaths forcing Lipton to do as they wished did not react.

Chapter 20

Samantha Black staggered as her last attack went nowhere. The level of focus on the boy by her team should have taken him down, but he stood. Their energy stores dropped below 25 percent. A bit late she realized she might have helped herself if she had reviewed some of the older reports about battle strategy or checked the specific accounts concerning the Sutter family. She paid the price for her laziness.

The unconscious, riveted kinetics lay where they dropped. Samantha ignored them. They were always the weak link in any strategy. All the mental attacks met an equal strength in defense or deflection. No mind assault had come from the boy. Samantha considered this to be significant: the key. Maybe he could not attack as she could; maybe he was good at defense but weak on offense. Maybe it was his mother who killed her jailor.

Of course, she thought, *it was the mother, never the boy.* This insight took on the aspect of obvious truth. Second-guessing was not a valuable trait to Samantha.

"You have done well." Samantha smiled as she gave Jason credit. "We obviously made mistakes. I underestimated you." She signaled her team to back off and regroup. She stepped back closer to the steel beam behind her. *Perhaps you missed a few things too.*

The shock of losing all of their kinetics in one fell swoop paralyzed Samantha's team. Their spirits dove as their hostage strategy devolved into illusion. How did the boy do it? The normals slept unaware and out of the way. It was not worth the energy expenditure to bring them back into the battle. In the midst of a moment's despair, they discovered a normal mind floors below. Two foot soldiers wrestled away his free will. Samantha witnessed the action telepathically and provided the strategy: kill Elizabeth Sutter in front of her son.

Lipton clutched his chest, breathing hard. He leaned on the rail and smiled at Harry Wyatt, who had come down the steps to assist.

"Just trying to catch my breath." Lipton coughed. "Russ needs you downstairs." He took several quick, deep breaths. "I'll stand guard here."

"What about Russ?" Harry stepped toward Lipton to help him take a seat on the steps.

The knife hidden behind Lipton's back came forward and plunged into Harry repeatedly. He stepped back. Bright-red streaks stained the front of his shirt, Harry collapsed against the wall. In shock, blood flowing from the wounds, he sank to the floor.

Lipton stood, flipped the knife in the air, and caught it by the handle. "Not so hard after all." He looked up and faced Elizabeth. "Let's take a walk."

She smiled.

Jason stood his ground. His eyes focused on the woman twenty feet away. His mind countered every telepathic attack efficiently. *I can do this all night.*

Elizabeth appeared to his right at the entrance to the stairwell. Lipton kept the blade visible and steady on her neck, just below her ear by her carotid artery. Death would be bloody but swift. Lipton pushed her forward onto the field of battle.

Elizabeth stood dignified, defiant. Her eyes were closed. Jason did not allow himself the luxury of a reaction.

Trust me. Come.

Without hesitation Jason entered a meditative state while standing; he floated inches above the floor. He intended to crush these people who threatened his mother. The world shifted.

"So nice of you to join me, dear." Elizabeth struggled to pull weeds in a heavily overgrown garden. Under a big, bright-red, wide-brimmed hat she looked up at her son. Her gloved hands struggled with large wads of bracken flailing like tentacles; they were trying to reconnect to the earth. "Come help. It will make the job go so much faster."

"I thought . . ." Jason could not complete his terrible thought.

"Have faith, son." Elizabeth stood up and tossed the garden waste into separate rusted garbage cans. "You start there with that big one. It has no place in my garden." She pointed to a large, treelike plant about three feet high. "Go deep and get the roots."

Jason stared at her; his feet refused his command. He could feel the cold steel as if it lay against his neck. She smiled.

"It is a small thing." Elizabeth waved her hand, dismissing the life-and-death scenario. She turned back to her endeavors. Jason regained motion and stood before the offending plant.

With a firm grip on the one-inch-thick stem, Jason heaved with all his strength. The plant lifted from the earth, but the roots pulled back. Jason went to his knees and released the stem. Quick as lightning, he got a hand on the left root, then on another to the right. He used the strength of his legs to stand. The roots relinquished the black soil, yet they stretched further on either side. Jason realized that this strategy was not going to break the connection. The plant was too deeply embedded.

Russ's voice echoed in his mind. "What'd I tell ya, all superhero and stuff." Jason grinned.

An S appeared on Jason's chest, along with blue tights on his legs. The costume faded in and out. Heat vision blasted from his eyes, slicing a root and cauterizing it to its core. The other shriveled and pulled away before he could deal with it.

"I think we are done here." Jason glanced over at his mother. She was no longer there.

The high-pitched shriek behind Samantha concerned her. She turned and watched as one of her team checked a body stretched on the floor; his hand sought a pulse at her neck.

"She's dead, Samantha." Dark circles grew under his eyes. "The boy killed her and pushed me out." He began to cry.

Samantha scorned his weakness; she could not even remember the name of the dead soldier. Another went to his knees. Weakness and failure were new experiences to her and her team.

"Not enough energy," complained the crier.

Jason settled to the floor, coming out of his meditation.

"I couldn't," choked Lipton, who had held the knife to Elizabeth's throat. He collapsed to his knees at Elizabeth's fee.

Samantha turned at the normal's protestations and watched him squirm, begging Elizabeth for forgiveness. Tears rolled down his cheeks. "I'm sorry. I am so sorry . . . How could I have?" he moaned.

Elizabeth knelt beside Lipton and whispered in his ear. He stretched out on the floor and fell into a deep sleep. She stood and faced Samantha.

Samantha returned her attention to Jason and found his eyes fixed on her. Though unsettled by the intensity, Samantha could not look away. Fury blazed in her enemy's eyes.

The offending knife lay on the floor by the normal. From the corner of her eye, she saw it fly across the few feet into Jason's hand. It rolled in his fingers; the polished steel reflected the ambient light as it turned. Too late, she now understood the power she faced.

The kinetic, one eye ruined and blood oozing from the wound, regained consciousness. Weak and confused on the cold concrete, he raised his head and watched the boy float and then settle to his feet. Time stood still. A six-inch nail lay a few feet away. Anger gave him strength. His closest friends lay crumbled on all sides. Revenge put a grin on his damaged face. The sharp sliver of steel rose a few feet and shot across the few yards directly at the boy's neck.

"Gotcha, ya little pri—" His head dropped. Consciousness slipped away.

The nail's point touched Jason's neck, and a half-inch circle of skin twirled open. The carotid artery moved dorsally a centimeter. The muscles made a path, while the trachea and esophagus moved slightly forward and back. The process repeated on the far side of Jason's neck. As the steel intruder passed, the tissues closed undamaged. The steel beam on the far side of Jason stopped the nail.

The sudden flash of sparks as metal impacted metal and the sound of the ricochet surprised Samantha. She broke contact with Jason and stared at the spot where the nail had struck. She analyzed the attack: a kinetic took the shot, and it should have worked. The boy should be on the ground, blood pooling around his head. It should have worked, but it didn't. He stood.

It was clear to Samantha that one more all-out attack might be possible. Like the German Panzer tanks in World War II waiting on their side of the Ardennes to begin the Battle of the Bulge, she prepared for her final push. Before her thought completed, the knife in Jason's hand shot out and plunged into her left shoulder. She grunted with the sudden pain. With intense scrutiny she studied the blade as it slowly withdrew, covered in her blood. She gasped at the intense pain.

As the point cleared, it drifted lower. In shock, Samantha thought the bright-red pattern on the steel was beautiful. The steel plunged again up to the hilt. It punctured her left lung and then pulled out. It hovered over her right side as she fell to her knees. The sharp blade floated down with her. She could not stop it. Blood filled her lung; some spilled over her lip when she coughed, trying to breath. Another strike ensured her death.

Samantha raised her head, confused, and looked up as the boy advanced. Jason knelt, reached over the hovering blade, and gently wiped the blood dripping from her chin with his finger. Their eyes locked once again.

Your choice: life or death?

The elevator gates clanged open. Harry Wyatt was carried in and settled on Jason's bed. Jason had stabilized him in the stairwell. The battlefield, however, was not the place for delicate repairs.

"Use me!" insisted Russ. He kept pressure on the knife wounds, though the bleeding had stopped. "I feel fine."

The others crowded around the bed. A few looked up when they heard Rodney coming down the iron stairs.

"What happened?" Rodney never got an answer. He looked over Downing's shoulder at the man on the bed. "Lost a lot of blood." He looked at the group around him. They waited. "Where's the doctor?"

Jason came up next to Russ and placed his hand on Harry's forehead. He closed his eyes and went to work. The cuts and nicks to the intestines closed; a duct-tape construct worked perfectly. The bacteria in the escaped excrement in his abdomen cavity, however, needed special treatment. A million of him with shovels cleaned the area. To handle the deadly bacteria, the million using shovels became millions with cattle prods that cauterized any colony found.

Jason gently lifted Russ's hands from his dad's wounds. They were well on their way to healing. He turned to his friend, nodded, and then watched as the exhaustion hit and he slid toward the floor. Chiang caught Russ, lifted his inert body in his arms, and placed him on a cot.

As Chiang help his friend, Jason caught Rodney's stare. He turned and addressed everyone.

"Harry is out of immediate trouble. He needs to rest, as do you all." Jason signaled Rodney to join him in the kitchen. To keep watch, Downing and Chiang pulled their cots closer to where Harry slept. The women, except for Elizabeth and Suzy, climbed the stairs to their waiting cots. Seth and his mother hovered within hearing distance of the kitchen.

"What happened, Mr. Sutter?" asked Rodney. "How many faced you? Who is left to fight another day? I assume, of course, that you won." He leaned his hip against the counter and crossed his arms. Suzy pulled herself up and sat on the counter opposite the stove. Elizabeth stood by her son.

"We won," Jason said. "There were about thirty-five or so. Some died; most didn't." Jason reached up, opened the cabinet door, and grabbed a glass. Rodney had to step back so Jason could filled it from the faucet. Jason drank half and then offered it to Suzy, who took it. She drank and then passed it to Elizabeth, who finished it.

"How did it all unfold, Mr. Sutter?!" Rodney almost yelled. Then he whispered, "How do normals survive like this?"

Jason read the intensity of Rodney's frustration with having no psychic abilities.

"Your plan worked well, Mr. Davenport." Jason took the empty glass from his mother and placed it in the sink. "I made a mistake. Dr. Lipton was captured and used to attack Russ's dad." Jason looked Rodney in the eye. "My mom and I took care of it."

"So easy? It couldn't have been that easy." Rodney looked from one face to the other. "Casualties?"

"All of the kinetics, several telepaths, a few seers," said Elizabeth. "Mostly wounded, but a few did not make it."

"Theirs?"

"Theirs, Rodney," Elizabeth said. She placed her hand on her son's shoulder.

"Samantha wasn't much ready for a knife fight," said Suzy.

"They faced my son with the intent to kill." Jason took a step back to allow his mother to step forward and confront the former leader of the Northeast Community. "With a little help, he crushed them. What else, Rodney, do you need to know?"

Jason monitored the wheels turning in the old man's head. Rodney Davenport, like Samantha Black, understood what stood before him.

"You, Mr. Davenport, unlike Ms. Black, are not too late to adjust your thinking."

Lipton had entered the apartment with the team but immediately, zombielike, peeled off from the group and collapsed onto his cot. He slept dreamless throughout the night and into the afternoon. He awoke with his memories fully intact.

"It's about time," said Jason. He sat with his arms resting on a chair back; his chin rested on his arm. "You missed both breakfast and lunch."

"Why don't you hate me?" The good doctor swung his legs over the edge of the cot. He held his hand to his head, forlorn. "I knifed Mr. Wyatt and might have done the same to your mother."

"Number one, you were outmatched. The choice was stripped from you. Harry is recovering nicely. Russ may want to call you a few bad names, however." Jason stood, turned the chair around, and sat, leaning close to his friend. "Number two, you planted doubt in very fertile ground with your annoying questions, just like you used to do with me." Jason grinned. "It was a courageous fight you put up. A chink in the wall opened for my mother to exploit."

"Oh." Lipton took his eyes off the floor and looked up into Jason's face, which showed acceptance and forgiveness. He controlled his guilt.

"Besides, doctor, it was me who left you unprotected. They grabbed you because I left you hanging out on a limb by yourself." Jason extended his hand. "I am sorry."

Lipton almost shouted, "Except I told you not to enter my mind without my permission. You kept your word. I didn't think clearly about the possible consequences." Lipton took Jason's hands in both of his and held them tightly in silence. "I too must say I am sorry."

"You hungry?" asked Jason. He stood up as Lipton released his hand.

"Starved."

"My mother will have a few questions for you." Jason put his arm around Lipton's shoulder. "It can wait until you're back to your superbly annoying self."

The doctor's laughter echoed off the red brick walls.

Chapter 21

The mansion owned by Louise and Mary was a welcomed sight. Exhausted by the drive from New York City, Jason, those who fought with him, and some who battled against him filed through the tall mahogany doors. Those on the other side of the fight had read the writing on the wall: the Sutter's could not be beaten. Twenty former enemies had joined them.

In the solarium where the Downings had married, they gathered after dumping their bags in their rooms and splashing their faces with cold water in the bathroom. Jason's crew lounged comfortably; slouched on pillowed couches and easy chairs, shoes off, they relaxed. The new members, their former enemies, sat up straight or leaned forward in nervous, private conversations about their uncertain futures. They stared at Rodney, who shared a love seat with Louise Deloro. Could their former leader offer them safety from the inevitable counterattack from Central?

Jason sat between his mother and Suzy. He relinquished Suzy's hand and took the floor. "We've arrived safe and sound." He scanned the room of smiling and frowning faces. "Okay, let's talk about the new people." In jeans and a black-and-white flannel shirt, and recently having turned fifteen, Jason realized that he projected a less than inspiring image. "You . . .

"Why are our abilities blocked?" asked a young man from the back.

"Because we do not know you." Jason put his hands in his pockets and shrugged, knowing that should have been obvious.

Jason went on. "Mr. Davenport continues to be blocked." He looked over his shoulder and nodded to his mother. "You will have to earn our respect, but you are alive. What would Miss Black have done?" The whispered words carried through the room: we'd be dead.

"Why here?" asked a woman. "Why not stay in New York?"

"New York was not defensible." Jason started to walk among the gathering. "A castle, so to speak, can be built here. We will need your help." He stopped in front of the young man with the first question. "It was a Petersburg maneuver."

"Ha!" laughed Downing. "Brilliant."

"A what?" asked the woman.

"This is why you lost." Jason addressed his former enemies. "You're lazy in your thinking, arrogant in your actions, and inflexible in your planning. All these things will change if you're on our team. You should know about the normals' history. We are part of it, whether they know of our existence or not." The room got quiet; all stared as though they were mesmerized by a candle flame.

"What will Central do?" The question hung in the air.

"Rodney?" Jason signaled for the old man to rise.

Still stiff, his body failed to cooperate fully. As he struggled, two hands landed on his hips and shoved him up. He swung around and faced Louise Deloro. "Thank you? I think," he stuttered.

"You're welcome," she said with a knowing grin.

Rodney stared at her for a second and then turned to the room. "You know me."

Jason moved to the edge of the gathering, watching Rodney recover some dignity. Rodney moved among the newcomers: his former troops. "I ask you to think about what happened. Thirty-five faced five: three immature seers and two telepaths. The kinetics were on your side, with none on the other."

"Yeah, but we couldn't see them. We can't fight what our minds can't see," said a twenty-something male who sat on the floor, leaning back against the couch where his fellow fighters had gathered. "And someone with telekinetic ability was there. Who controlled the knife?"

Rodney said, "You're right on your first point . . . Jack, isn't it?" The man nodded. "Jack, do you think after you analyze the battle that the outcome would have changed if the knife was never used? You believed, for example, you had flesh and blood, normal hostages out in front? Your belief was used against you as the real normals were taken off the field by Mr. Sutter." His statement met stunned silence.

Rodney went to Jason's side and put a hand on his shoulder. "Remember that this boy and his mother"—he pointed to Elizabeth—"know everything there is to know about you and me." He slowly scanned the group. "Yet you and me—especially me—are still alive. That, ladies and gentlemen, is strength: a complete lack of fear. Besides, I don't know of any one of us who can do what this young man can."

Rodney continued. "It was Mr. Sutter who controlled the knife. Consider the implications." He looked at Jason and said, "That is power."

Stunned silence fell on the room.

Jason broke the silence. "It's a lot to consider. No one will be forced to join us. Our plan is to gather as many in the Northeast Community willing to build a new Community here. All will become warriors to the best of their talents: no farmers, if ya know what I mean."

"Will Central give us time?" asked Jack.

Rodney replied, "They will need about two or three months to position and fortify the attack. They will enter New York City with an overwhelming force and find it an empty fortress. We have that long, plus the time it will take to find out where we went." Rodney hesitated and asked Jason, "Will they find you?"

"Certainly." Jason looked at his mother, who shrugged. "When they know, I guess, is my call. I haven't made it yet."

Rodney returned to his seat.

"Do you believe anything you just said?" whispered Louise in Rodney's ear. Jason overheard and saw Rodney smile at her.

"Most of it." Rodney glanced at Jason. "We can discuss the part I don't believe later, if you wish." Louise smiled and nodded.

Rodney's reaction to Louise amused Jason. The former leader decided he would either terminate this normal's life when he regained his abilities or, more likely, would find her indispensable. He liked her, which he found to be an unexpected, revolting development.

"I, for one, am bushed," called out Downing. "Talk among yourselves. We can get together and continue over dinner." Without much thought, some rose to their feet and moved out of the solarium. Jason went to Suzy, and together they headed upstairs to check on the Wyatts.

✳   ✳   ✳

Reena hung up the wall phone. "It has started." She took a seat at the table after she filled a mug with freshly brewed coffee and pulled a spoon from a drawer.

"I'm sure it will be very successful." Bill's tone suggested he believed the opposite.

"Okay, dear." Reena added sugar to her coffee. She smiled patiently. "What's on your mind?"

"With your help I have been able to see how nothing went as I thought in Pennsylvania." Bill gathered his thoughts carefully. He could not stand how his partner had isolated herself from him since his return. "Perhaps we need to consider that they possess a strategy that will thwart ours. What would that look like? Should we work a backup, a Plan B, if this first effort yields nothing useful?"

Reena reached out, ran her fingers through his hair, and patted his shoulder in a reassuring manner as she said, "The sweep will give us back New York. The New Englanders will follow. The enemy will be isolated and slowly strangled. Time, my dear, is on our side."

✳   ✳   ✳

There was a knock at the door, and a moment later Jason and Suzy appeared. Russ threw his arms around them. "That's twice, man," he whispered—his sister and his father saved. "We may have to buy you a Christmas present or something."

"I expected to find him on death's door." Jason heard Peg Wyatt say over his shoulder. He turned. She was relaxing in a rattan chair, watching her husband devouring a big bowl of chocolate ice cream. "Like a kid after a tonsillectomy." Harry gave her a big grin and shoveled more in his mouth.

"How's he doin', Russ?" asked Jason.

"When he woke up, he made some stupid joke about getting the attention he deserved. I knew then he was okay." Russ looked back at his father on the bed. "When the ice cream arrived, you would have thought he'd won a lot of money. You don't want to hear his joke about that."

"Did you fill your mom in on what is happening?" asked Suzy.

"Not yet, but . . ." Russ sighed, "she has a surprisingly good idea about what is going on."

Jason and Suzy left Russ to explain things to his mother and went in search of Frank, their foster father. They found him sitting alone in the living room—a large, grand space with heavy mahogany furniture. Bookshelves covered one wall, floor to ceiling, and Frank sat in an easy chair with his feet up on an ottoman.

"Can you believe it?" Frank held up the book he was reading when Jason asked him how he was doing. "A signed copy! Can you believe it?" He showed them the title page. The name, George Orwell, was clearly scrawled on the page.

"Frank?" Jason said. "I think we owe you an explanation of what has been happening."

Frank looked at his foster son. "Jason, I firmly believe that you have done what you had to do. Apparently there were some serious goings-on in New York City." His gaze moved from one to the other. "You both are here safe and sound. I am glad. You . . ." he pointed at Jason, "and your mother. You are no longer an orphan." He closed the book and put it on his lap. "My world has been kinda turned upside down but . . ." He stood, went to the shelves, and replaced the book with great care. "What do you need me to know and how can I be of further help to you?"

Jason told Frank the whole story. Suzy added more details where needed.

"I will be building something big, Frank." Jason put out his hand as Frank had done when Jason left for New York. "I want you to be part of it. I think I can use all the kids at the house. We will need places for new people to stay. What do you think? Can you help?"

"Yes." Frank took Jason's hand and shook it. "Will you be coming back to the house tonight?"

"I think, Frank," said Jason, looking at Suzy, "that a number of us will be returning to the house tonight."

Two hours later, Jason, Suzy, and Russ sat at the tool bench in the shed behind the Dubois house. Two more stools had to be found and more candles as the daylight retreated. Elizabeth and Rodney had joined the children.

"Rather humble beginnings," Rodney said. He squirmed a bit on the unpadded stool; it had no Christmas wrapping paper like the others.

"Watch out for the splinters," Russ said from experience, leaning close to the old man.

"A little sandpaper might help." Rodney raised himself off the hard seat and brushed away bits and pieces. Russ smiled and nodded.

"Okay," said Jason, addressing the adults. "What now?" Shadows from the lit candles danced on the walls. A cool breeze blew through the open door.

"As soon as possible," Rodney said, "we need to get our agents up to the New England outposts, so to speak, and get those people down here."

"What?" Jason asked.

"There is a crescent of Community groups in the northeast that runs from Upstate New York to Cape Cod." Elizabeth looked witchlike staring into the candle as its light played on her face; an incantation seemed imminent. "These are the noncombatants. They would be like the Amish in the American Civil War: against slavery but not willing to pay the violent price needed to end it."

"How many?" asked Suzy.

"A thousand or so." Rodney yawned. He rubbed his eyes and then stretched. "The day, it seems, has worn me down."

Jason was shocked by the number. "Who will be our agent to bring them here?"

"Rodney, of course," stated Elizabeth. "He has already set up his team for the embassy."

Jason faced his mother. "So you have decided to release him?"

"Yes, dear." Elizabeth's lips turned up in an exhausted smile. "I think he has earned it."

As Elizabeth explained herself, a silk-tethered spider landed on Russ's hand. The tickling drew his attention. He transferred the eight-legged shed inhabitant to Suzy, who chuckled.

"Remember how we found out that Jason floated when he meditated?" She set the spider's path to Jason, who welcomed the beast. He held up his hand as the creature climbed to his fingertips. Then he brought his hand slowly to the table surface. The spider froze a moment on the wood surface; warmth beckoned to it.

Without hesitation, the spider's front legs sought a place on Rodney's thumb. As it climbed up and sought his palm, Rodney brought the bug closer for examination. The animal killed and ate to survive; it had young as often as it could but didn't care about its children. The spider's existence mirrored Rodney's.

Rodney stood and walked to a corner of the toolshed; the spider rapidly crawled away to its web. "I should go soon," said Rodney.

"You will be released tomorrow," said Elizabeth. "It is time to release all who have sacrificed so much for us."

Chapter 22

The time had come.

Jason sat across from his mother beneath the great oak tree in the bird sanctuary. It was there that Jason had stumbled into Chiang Chen, his good friend. It was there he felt most safe and there he had performed his early outlandish feats of psychic skill. It would be there that the cover would be removed from the locked box. The captive would be launched from certain safety.

As they walked into the park, Jason pointed out the places where his psychic insight and growth had occurred. The sound of gurgling water falling over stones filled the air. Jason explained that it was Chiang's project; he had used the Dubois inmates to bring the fountain and surrounding garden back to life.

Beneath the spreading bows of the great tree, their knees touched as they sat cross-legged on the ground. Elizabeth reached up and grasped either side of her son's head.

The half-empty cup that was Jason Sutter filled. All his memories returned to his synapses and nodes. His brain made room without disturbing his knowledge of the world in the Dubois house. He remembered. It was trivial until he opened his eyes and saw his mother's face.

Time shifted. They were knee to knee in a rundown house, running away from their tormentors. The tears on his mother's face flashed in his mind. He was beneath an old oak tree, and he wasn't.

Jason gave up—to hell with reality—and truth from the past flooded his present. He could not exist another second without his arms clinging to his mother, and so it was. Beneath an old tree he cried about his launch into family betrayal and return: the prodigal mother had returned to the abandoned child. The healing, as their minds entwined and knew like no other knowing who they were, began in earnest.

Six weeks prior to Jason and his mother touring the bird sanctuary, Rodney's powers were in full bloom when he approached the New England groups. Louise joined him at every confrontation. Sometimes Rodney had her stand before a small crowd and describe her part in the demise of the warriors in New York. They never remained in one place for more than a day or two. It was not safe.

There were moments when Louise felt completely ignored. She would describe to Jason on her return the meetings with somber persons who never spoke a word; the next day they were all smiles. She could not comprehend the psychic give and take going on. Louise would recall with great detail how Rodney had treated her with the utmost respect and caring throughout their travels. She would eventually confess to her sister, Mary, that Rodney might love her in his way.

Two weeks after Jason came to know his mother, hundreds of new people arrived in Franklin Chase needing shelter and safety—a surety that they would survive.

"Well, Miss Deloro," said Rodney one afternoon when a group of twenty arrived, "it would appear that we did our jobs very well."

"Did we?" Louise watched from a window as the small caravan of cars unloaded their travelers. It was cold outside; the windows had frost at their corners. She turned from the view. "What now, Mr. Rodney Davenport?"

The words and the wave of energy coming from Louise caught Rodney unprepared. He was not a target; Louise possessed no ability. Her feelings came to him when he looked; he had opened the door. She made his travels to remote areas surprisingly pleasant and presented him with a worldview different from his own. His prejudice against normals had hamstrung his appreciation of the obvious for too long. He liked her.

"I do not understand what has happened to me." Rodney became very serious. "I have done evil in the name of self-preservation. I would continue to do so if not for what?" He shook his head. "Perhaps Jason had something to do with it. He has been in and around the inside of my head since they found me in that alley." He stared out the window, not wanting to look at Louise. "I am different now . . . I guess."

"Again, Mr. Rodney Davenport, what do we do now?" Louise said.

Rodney looked at her and saw acceptance. He took a deep breath and smiled. "We dance, Miss Deloro." Rodney opened his arms, inviting her in. "We dance."

She fell into his arms. "You could have made this a little easier, you know."

If I weren't such a fool! In the silence of the room, the Blue Danube played in their minds.

Louise caught her breath as his words entered her mind. She smiled. *We will be fools together.*

✶   ✶   ✶

Reena Sorenson considered the situation. On her porch, wrapped in a blanket, she engaged her sonar. Bill, a seer, yelled that something was happening. Energy exploded on her awareness. The obvious power in Pennsylvania needed no explaining. It was the boy. Reena studied the power signature from her front porch in North Dakota. The brightness almost obscured all other inputs. The boy was not alone. A few new warriors did not concern her. The power around the boy did not give her pause. She monitored what was happening in New York as the assault began. It was a supremely wasted effort.

With great concentration, Reena absorbed Jason Sutter. No hiding anymore. She found Elizabeth Sutter as well. In a fit of frustration and fury, she realized they saw her also. They welcomed the awareness.

Come and get us, they teased. Their laughter bounced around in Reena's mind.

Furious, she pulled the blanket closer and doubled her effort. She pulled back from her singular focus on Jason and Elizabeth. Others with abilities registered. One, two, three became hundreds slowly rising into the night sky over a city. As she went higher, countless lights became bright rivers; they spread and network in all directions.

Reena broke contact. The effort in New York had to be stopped. It was too late; the Pennsylvania fortress glowed with hard, battle-ready troops patrolling the virtual walls. The New York Community was no more. The complete break with Central meant that the revolution continued. The interim years were a respite before finishing the fight.

Reena powered down. She noticed Bill, who leaned against the porch rail breathing heavily. Ignoring his condition, she shivered beneath her blanket, with defeat hanging like a lead apron on her. Reena was afraid. She escaped the chair and the blanket, and paced the porch.

"Who will stop the normals from overrunning us?" She stopped, stomped her feet, daring Bill to interrupt. "Who will stop the annihilation of our kind? Don't they see that they will destroy us?!"

Bill, always calm, faced his partner of many decades and said, "They know the risk, not the certainty." He put his hands on her shoulders and locked her eyes with his. "Let them have their experiment. When it fails, you win; the normals destroy them. We make sure their downfall does not touch the rest of us."

She said nothing. Bill gently turned her around, and they went into their home.

The next day scouts were assigned to monitor the new Community, looking for the normals to do what they did so well. What normals misunderstood, they killed.

☆   ☆   ☆

The new couples and the few couples with children from New England sought sanctuary in Franklin Chase. Frank Dubois provided lodging, as did Mary and Louise. A more permanent solution forced Jason into a real-estate mogul job. He conferred with contractors and arranged for homes to be built in the hundreds. When complete, Jason wiped his name from every normal person with whom he dealt.

"Now what?" asked Suzy.

"I'm not sure." Jason sat back. It was just the two of them in the toolshed on a sunny afternoon in November. Thanksgiving approached. There was much to be thankful for, in Jason's opinion. Still the not-so-subtle demand on him to be king from Russ, Rodney, and his mother continued. He struggled with the notion of American liberty while a strong enemy watched for weakness.

That morning, sitting with Russ in the kitchen at his house, Rodney and his mother had arrived unexpectedly and confronted him.

"It would be best," Elizabeth said, getting right to the point, "if you would take on the mantle of leadership for this entire Community." She looked worried. "You have been overheard to say something about voting for a leader."

"I concur," said Rodney. "Lack of firm leadership on your part at this juncture may unhinge everything you have built so far." Rodney pointed at Jason. "You cannot leave us to the free-for-all confusion and chaos of democracy. We simply are not strong enough yet."

Jason did not speak. He waited for Russ to argue the point.

"History," said Russ, shrugging his shoulders, "is full of failed kingdoms, 'cause the guys leading the show get all moral about taking power and walked away."

"Until Reena is neutralized," Elizabeth said, "we look to you to set the strategy. You must take charge and play the leading role."

Jason stuttered, "I . . . I will think on it."

"I can't be the king." Jason combed his fingers through his hair, trying to think. "I'm not gonna let the Community look weak and let the other Communities attack in a long string of Pyrrhic victories and defeats."

"So?" asked Suzy.

"I'll be temporary king to settle big things with, ya know, you and the Franklin Chase crew. The lesser issues can be delegated to groups to vote on . . . You hungry?"

Suzy shook her head and asked, "You goin' back to school? Should I prepare for life in New York City?"

"Yeah, I want to." Jason scratched his chin. "There is so much I don't know." He paused. "There is time to work that out."

Jason took her hand, and they left the shed. Halfway across the yard, Suzy abruptly stopped and pulled on Jason's arm, turning him. She stood on tiptoe, her arms went around his neck, and she kissed him. When their lips parted, the single greatest psychic on the face of the Earth smiled embarrassed like any first-kissed, teenage boy. Not sure what to do next, he kissed her again.

It's good to be normal.

☆ ☆ ☆

"Jackie-O!" The green pickup truck honked twice as it slowed and flashed its headlights. Jack O'Malley pushed away from his taxi, where he had been leaning, drinking coffee. He turned to the street and laughed.

"Hunter!" He raised the steaming Styrofoam cup in salute.

"Working too hard there, Jackie." The smiling, bearded face leaned out of the window as it passed the yellow cab waiting in front of the Franklin Chase train station. The huge, brass pedestal clock in front of the station chimed ten times. The blinking decorations up and down the street lit up the night.

"Gotta keep Christmas merry!"

"Roger that, Jack." Hunter waved as he picked up speed and then yelled a Merry Christmas as he took the next right and disappeared from view.

Jack settled back against his taxi. It was getting colder. The hot coffee helped. He pulled his policeman-like cap lower on his head. A prayer went into the night that the ten-oh-five heading to Philadelphia would be on time. The answer came when the train arrived five minutes early.

The woman in the blue dress beneath the short, gray wool coat and high heels looked familiar. Jack noted the large suitcase in her right hand—kitchen-sink heavy, as he recalled. The severe expression and pulled-back hair placed her in his memory. He gulped the rest of his coffee. As he tossed the cup into the garbage can, she came up and handed him her luggage. It was unexpectedly light. *Welcome back*, hung on the tip of his tongue, but he knew it would not be appreciated.

"Still needs makeup," he whispered as he opened the trunk and tossed in the bag. With the luggage stowed and passenger onboard, Jack started the engine. "Where to?"

"49 Hickory Lane."

Jack pulled into traffic and kept his thoughts to himself.

Lydia Dubois kept silent as well. She stared out at the sameness of Franklin Chase as the taxi wove its way through the streets. She smiled. The suitcase without the cash made the return trip more manageable. She patted the black leather purse that kept the cashier's check nestled with cash in a clip. Lydia envisioned a triumphant return.

"Stop!" Her sudden outburst shocked Jack, who hit the brakes. They were thrown forward.

"I'll get out here." Lydia was out of the back seat before the car came to a full stop at the curb.

With the car in park, Jack jumped out and put the suitcase on the sidewalk. The taxi idled half a block away from the large Victorian house. He jumped back behind the wheel with the ten-dollar tip grasped in his hand and rushed away.

Lydia gaped from the safety of a tree's shadow. Not everything in Franklin Chase remained the same. The house, her house, blazed with Christmas lights. The cold pushed her from hiding. On the walkway, bag in hand, she felt small before the great house decked out in celebration; she hated it. With eyes closed, determined, Lydia Dubois stepped forward into the light.

Epilogue

≁

March 1965

Reverend Steve Conner leaned on the window ledge and stared through the open blinds. He looked for the sun to offer light from the distant horizon. From the second floor of his small house, he waited for the snow-covered farmer's fields to rise from the darkness. The black sky paled slowly. The tree-lined plots emerged and stretched from the feet of the mountains into the plains. Time passed, and the barest arc of red crawled into the gray sky. Long shadows pointing west revealed the barns and houses.

Steve witnessed the growing light and prayed for guidance. He needed a sign from the loving God in whom he believed. The vivid dreams had disrupted his sleep more often in the last weeks. What did they mean? Memories, once clear, faded.

Steve showed up in Red Oak, Colorado, in 1948, after the big storm. Red Oak nestled between the Rockies foothills and the Great Plains. Nature's violence almost destroyed the town, the farms, and the folks caught up in its terror. The town's barber, Red Martin, survived and he did not hesitate to tell every customer still standing that he did not expect the town to recover. It did. The influential locals, like Red; Sally Thurman, who owned Joe's Diner; Jordan Crass, who would become the town's mayor; and most of the surviving farmers, believed their rise from the disaster was due to the presence of Reverend Conner.

For years after the storm, they gathered regularly at Joe's. Sally kept the coffee mugs filled. Loud voices argued the common-sense logic of what happened. Their rebirth could not be explained to everyone's satisfaction. It wasn't like the reverend did anything. He quoted the Bible, chapter and verse from his storefront church in the early years. He finished his sermons with, "Help will come for those who help themselves. God is a caring God. Let us pray." Conner dropped his head and sought salvation in a near-empty room.

Good things, however, started happening. Government disaster relief poured into Red Oak. The local farmers as well as businessmen and their families worked together to rebuild each other's farms. Amazed at their success, they planted that year's crop against all the odds. Hope grew, and Reverend Conner preached across the plains, going farm to farm with God's word. He learned about the needs of his flock and admonished those who had more to give.

"Step up and do God's work," he demanded.

They did. Red Oak blossomed as the storefront church attracted overflow crowds at Sunday services. The town decided that Reverend Conner needed a reason to put down roots in their small town. They built him a church.

The walls and roof of Christ's Love Church were raised on a Wednesday and the doors opened for services the following Sunday. Steve expressed his thanks to the townsfolk and praised God's will. The following Monday, the bankers relaxed their financial demands on all the farmers of Red Oak. The recovery stopped dead in its tracks as the community tried to figure out why the predators were suddenly changing their cutthroat ways.

Always under the boot of the bankers, the small landholders started to think something else was creating this largess. They relaxed when it came to light that Congress had given the vultures in the three-piece suits a special tax incentive. The attendees drinking coffee at Joe's felt more secure. If the bankers found God's grace, then surely frogs might rain from the sky.

Steve turned from the window as the sun's full disc climbed over the horizon. His wife, Annie, slept soundly. Quiet as a cat, he padded from the room with a shirt, jeans, and socks. He changed in the bathroom and then went to the kitchen. With the percolator cleaned and ready, a strong pot of coffee was soon bubbling merrily. Steve leaned against the counter and waited for the rising water to turn black.

Reverend Conner looked thirty-something years old. His parishioners thought he was older. His calm demeanor and sage advice gave that impression. With a day's growth of beard and unruly, thick, brown hair he drank his first of many mugs of coffee. The dark circles under his blue eyes had begun to worry the whole town.

He sat at the kitchen table thinking. The Lord had reached out and touched him. As a child, Steve saw things that no one else did.

As he stared straight ahead, sipping his coffee, the memory of standing on a foldout chair beneath the great revival tent played in his mind's eye. He was six years old. His mother had dragged Steve to the service; she craved such "Come to Jesus" services. At the time they lived in California, near Modesto in the Central Valley.

Resting his hand on his mother's shoulder, going up on tiptoe, Steve wanted to see if the people were the same as last time. He searched the field of adoring faces, thirsty for the Word. All eyes fixed on the stage. Some of the people glowed yellow, red, or green. The child smiled and would have giggled if not for the outburst of Preacher Murcock.

"Sinners, beware!"

Steve turned around and fixed his eyes on the gray-haired, dark-eyed, old man standing above him.

"Philistines! God crushed the demons with the strong right arm of the Israelites!" Spittle flew over the stage; Murcock pounded the podium. "The blood of the unbelievers, the fornicators, the blasphemers covered the battlefield." The gray head dropped. The charged silence excited the crowd. They leaned forward as one, afraid they might miss something.

"You!" the preacher cried out. He glared and pointed an accusing finger across the gathering. "All of you! No innocence here!" He glared for an instant at the boy standing above the crowd. Steve gulped, captured by the old man's wide-eyed, crazy stare.

"Some of you have joined the Philistine camp. Some of you are thinking about going over to the enemy." Murcock's eyes slowly moved from the boy to every section of his audience. "Don't deny it! You know who you are!" He paused. "Do not go into the darkness! How many of you have forsaken the Lord's light to satisfy your devil's urges in the serpent's nest of Los Angeles!"

Released from the preacher's fiery eyes, Steve looked behind him. The people still glowed.

"Forsake the darkness and come into the light of sweet Jesus's love." He paused. In that gap, a small, six-year-old voice carried the length and breadth of the tent.

"I see people with light."

Steve smiled as he sat in his kitchen. His simple statement of fact had started his career as God's tool, which brought him step-by-step from the small towns in the Central Valley of California to Red Oak. Murcock was probably more interested in his mother but took the boy under his wing. Steve learned a great deal from the man about the Bible, God, and showmanship; Murcock became the father he never had. The boy was often trotted out to find the people of the light in the crowds as they rode the revival circuit in the late thirties.

Eventually Steve stopped seeing the glowing people. He finally broke out on his own when he turned eighteen. The old man and his mother stayed together until she died ten years ago. Steve heard that Murcock had died soon after. It bothered Steve that he had trouble remembering his mother's face. And where did they live when traveling with Murcock?

In the last few weeks, as he was being plagued by a recurring dream, his talent had returned: people glowed again. Confused, he wondered what God had in mind for him. With his elbows on the table and his head in his hands, he gave up his uncertainty and prayed.

The refrigerator door opened and closed, interrupting his meditations. He looked up.

"Couldn't sleep again?" Annie pulled a glass from the cabinet and filled it with milk. She turned to him, drinking, and then put the glass on the counter. She wiped her mouth on the sleeve of her flannel pajamas. "Same dream?"

"Yeah."

Even though she wore green plaid, oversized pajamas, Steve worshipped her beauty. Thick, dark brown hair flowed over her shoulders and framed her laughing green eyes, patrician nose, high cheekbones, and thick, velvet lips. In the midst of his troubles, he still wanted her.

"The Christmas light people are still chasing you?" She smiled over her shoulder when she turned to pull a pack of cookies from the shelf.

"Kinda." Steve tensed at the way she made a joke of his dream, but let it go. "But very dangerous lights. All I can do is run."

"Do they catch you?" Annie nibbled her cookie.

Steve's first reaction was to forget the whole thing and carry her back upstairs. His second was to give her an honest answer. "I am running very fast. I am a blur." He closed his eyes. "I am not alone. There are others running with me."

"Anyone you know?" She put the milk bottle back in the fridge.

"Hard to tell. The faces are hard to see. We are moving too fast." He rubbed his eyes and then finished his coffee. He stood and went to the stove to pour more. "Anyway," he said, filling the mug, "I always wake up when the glowing people are about to grab us." He looked at his wife and put down his cup and the percolator. Steve grabbed Annie around her waist and pulled her close. "Thanks for listening." He kissed her neck. She leaned into his caress.

"What time is your meeting today?" Annie leaned back and glanced at the clock over the fridge.

"Seven-thirty." He had forgotten about the meeting at the church, with his worries scrambling his emotions.

"You've got forty minutes." She pressed his cheeks between her hands and kissed him. "Off with you."

Thirty minutes later, showered and shaved, Steve headed into town to keep his appointment. Talk about building a grain elevator nearby became real when the money for the project became a reality. For decades the local farmers had hauled their crops two hundred miles to the closest elevator.

The new one would cut the distance to twenty miles. The townsfolk had dreamed of this and credited their reverend for his efforts and heavenly connections.

Steve parked in the empty church lot. He killed the engine and wondered if all the good fortune was God's hand. For some reason he had not told Annie about the dream's end and what brought him fully awake, unable to stay in bed. Winter's cold crept into the truck as he recalled the details of last night's dream.

There is a woman in a chair facing away from him. Her blonde hair is unkempt. He approaches and places his hand gently on her shoulder. Leaning over, close to the woman's ear, he whispers, "Now, Beth."

Startled awake, Steve choked on a great loss, a great sadness. Tears fell from his cheeks to the floor, unstoppable. In the bathroom the night before, he had tried to get control of himself with little success. *Who is Beth? What is this terrible loss?*

"God help me," he moaned. He had wiped his eyes with toilet paper and then waited at the window for the sun.

Another truck pulled into the lot and parked next to Steve. The driver waved hello and killed the engine.

"Morning, Jordie," called Steve, getting out of his truck. Jordan Crass, the duly elected mayor of Red Oak, walked over and clapped Steve on the back.

"Big day, Reverend. A very big day." Mayor Crass was a good soul clad in layers of extra pounds. He looked like a young Santa Claus with a bushy, dark brown beard.

Other vehicles turned into the lot as Steve unlocked the church doors. The men walked across the lot and glowed in Steve's eyes.

"Go ahead in, Jordie. I'll greet and welcome these folks."

"I'll get the coffee going." The mayor missed the reverend's intense, severe scrutiny of the men climbing the steps to his sanctuary. Smiling, ignoring the reverend's distrust, they shook his hand and passed into the church. *God, please, what is happening?*

Once Steve was in the meeting room, the auras disappeared. Shaken, he put aside his confusion and started the meeting with a heartfelt welcome and a prayer. These were the money men who would help the whole town. Steve's private concerns did not count.

The hour meeting ended successfully for Red Oak. The elevator construction would start in a few weeks. Steve missed most of the discussion, unable to focus. Jordie did all the work and kept the meeting moving forward.

Once the men were ushered out of the church and the doors were closed and locked from the inside, Steve went to the large, wooden cross hanging behind the podium. He spread his arms wide and went to his knees. The lights and auras had always been signs of God's touch. His dreams said otherwise. Which was the good? Which led to evil?

Confusion about the Word of God had never bothered Steve until now.

In Christ's Love Church, beneath the cross, with the doors closed and the windows sealed for the winter, a breeze touched Steve's cheek. "Ro . . . be . . . rt," echoed longingly in his mind as a soft, drawn-out whisper. Steve felt bereft; the mental caress reached deep into his bones. Last night's tears fell again.

About the Author

Jay Sherfey holds a Masters Degree in Electrical Engineering and closes on thirty years in the electronics industry. He has authored two books, "Misunderstood: Healing Jason Sutter" and "Misunderstood: Nothing to Joke About". He lives in Worcester, MA with his wife, Claudia, his two children, Kirstin and John, and their four pleasantly neurotic cats.